Harrison's Story

ISBN: 978-1-4583-0275-5

Edited by: David Repasky

Dedication

This book is dedicated to my parents, Bud and Kris, who have fought my battle with mental illness just as I have.

While the battle has been long and hard, it is with their dedication, support and effort that we have transformed what could have been the end into a new beginning.

Introduction

Dear Reader,

It is important to introduce the pages in this book as fiction. Harrison Remy is a character that I developed while in prison. Those were some very dark days, as one might imagine. I was not sure if I would make it through those days and the only thing that I could find that would bring comfort and hope, was Harrison.

I imagined a man that I wanted to be. I decided to incorporate my life along with so many others that I had met along the way into something positive and something to look forward to, in order to transcend the circumstance.

Do I believe that I will attain a level of success Harrison has? Not necessarily, however what is most important is that I am definitely on the path to attaining his level of awareness, the reality of the pages you are about to read is in fact my philosophy and my belief system.

There are no pages in this book that directly refers to any one person. Throughout the story of Harrison Remy, you will see what in reality is a collaboration of many responses and actions from my life and the hundreds of people I have met that have dealt with similar issues as they pertain to mental illness and diversity.

The first goal of the story of Harrison Remy was to help me survive. The second goal and reason that I published this book is in the hope that those dealing with similar issues can find hope, compassion and understanding for those living with mental illness and their loved ones. I also want those living with the circumstances and symptoms of mental illness to know that mental illness is maintainable – but it takes an army and a sincere determination.

It is also important to realize that I take full responsibility for my life and the behavior that has gone with it. Mental illness is not an excuse for bad behavior, however it is a reason and it is much more difficult to gain control of than one might think. While great strides are being made to correctly address the issues of mental illness and the criminal justice system, there is a long way to go. A great deal of the obstacles in front of us comes from the stigmatization and misunderstanding of mental illness.

In the back of this book you will find a list of resources if you are in need of any help.

The only request that I have when reading this book, is that you sit back, open your mind and gain perspective from one person's point of view. There will be things you do not agree with and things that you do and that is perfectly fine; this is how we grow.

Blessings,

Cory Dobbelaere

Today was a day made for nervousness. I was about to embark on a journey with Harrison Remy, a person I had long admired. I stood in the bathroom, getting ready to drive to his Michigan home, which was one of many that he owned. As I look in the mirror, I can see that the whites of my eyes were bloodshot, and the redness was an awful contrast to my brown eyes. I feel like I might have stayed up too late last night. I wasn't doing anything I shouldn't have, I was just tossing and turning thinking about all I had to do today. As I combed my hair, I noticed what looked like a few gray streaks mixed in with the brown. How could this be? I was only 22! As I got dressed, I wanted to make sure I looked my best. While not rich enough to wear Armani, I made enough to wear Armani Exchange. When I was dressed, I grabbed my bags, turned off the light and went out the door.

It was on a beautiful fall morning, in late September; that I turned onto the long, wooded drive. The trees were full of vibrant colors. As I drove down the lane, I watched the leaves fall slowly and peacefully through the air. The air was fresh and new. It seemed as though anyone would find this place a charming nirvana. As I weave my way down the private drive, my eyes turn to a beautiful, two-story log cabin – perfectly landscaped to match nature itself. The cabin displayed large wood pillars, providing a roof over a massive entry porch. With two rocking chairs scattered opposite each other, the porch

seemed inviting and cozy. As I pulled up to the cabin, I noticed a brick-laid sidewalk coming from the main house to the drive. As I looked to the right of the house, I could see a log pole barn equally landscaped. The grounds must be five acres of solid woods! The sun sparkled down through the trees as if Thomas Kinkade had created this reality himself.

I pulled my car to a stop and take a deep breath. I am 22 years old and about to meet an 80 year old man, who is nothing less than a legend in my mind. He is elusive and extremely private. I'd heard that in his younger days, he knew how to work any crowd. His personality radiated like electricity, bringing light to all the dark spaces. He was known to be feisty, opinionated and guarded; yet also known as one of the most compassionate people in the world. My name is Mason Turner and I am about to meet Mr. Harrison Remy, a writer, poet and advocate. Harrison wasn't a resume. You couldn't break down or easily categorize his accomplishments. No one really knew, but the man himself, how many back stories and keepsakes he was a part of. I knew most of it, or so I thought. But I couldn't have prepared myself for the moment that was taking place.

I drove from Chicago to this incredible private home in northern Michigan, nestled in the woods off the coast of Lake Michigan. It's a family home that Harrison had been coming to for the past 40 years.

Harrison is 80 years old now and still maintains residence in South Africa, Michigan, Ohio and New York City. The anticipation has been building for months. I have read every book, article, poem and report ever published about this extremely complex man. I step out of my car, and hear a man's voice welcoming me:

"I have prepared a room for you so bring along your bags."

I'm feeling both nervous and excited, as I wheel my suitcase to the porch; leading to the double doors of this large, but beautifully cozy home.

"It is so nice to meet you, sir" as I reach out to shake Mr. Remy's Hand.

Harrison is nearly six feet tall, and has silver hair, healthy tanned skin and piercing blue eyes. He is an attractive, sophisticated looking man, looking 60 years young and in good shape. Harrison grabs me and gives me a hug rather than the handshake and welcomes me.

"My name is Harrison and you may call me Harrison – I can't very well be on a professional level with someone who intends to write about my life, now can I?"

"I guess not."

"Let me show you your room, Mason."

The home is spectacular, yet practical. A large wooden staircase leads to the second floor, lit by the sun through a large skylight. Harrison opens a door and shows me into a spacious room, with a queen-size log bed and a dresser carved from natural wood. The sliding French doors open to a balcony overlooking a beautiful, wooded backyard. As I look, I notice a paved path that meanders down to a clear, flowing river. I can see two boats docked along the shore, opposite an exquisite 19th century Gazebo, from which any guest could have an inspiring view of the tranquil water.

"This is truly breathtaking," I say nearly speechless.

"We enjoy it here. It always helps to clear the mind. Mason, why don't you make yourself at home? There's no rush. Take your time unpacking. I will see you on the back deck in your time – the boys will show you the way – cheerio!" Harrison says.

While unpacking, I actually felt the warm sensation of excitement realizing that I was going to be spending time with Harrison Remy! He had dedicated his life to being a voice for those who did not have one. He utilized everything he had to make sure that understanding and education were provided for those with mental illness, and others that were so misunderstood. However, not one thing seems a bit pretentious about Harrison. The only strange thing I truly notice is how impeccable everything is – how organized and perfect.

Chapter 1

Day One with Harrison

As I walk down the stairs, sure enough, the boys are waiting at the bottom. "The boys" aren't Harrison's children. They're just Harrison's two favorite companions. He never goes anywhere without them. Taj and Dexter guide me down the sunlit entryway to the back of the house where six massive sliding French doors are open. I walk through the doors to see an incredible deck complete with a bar, built in grill and outdoor kitchen.

"This is incredible!"

"Thank you Mason," Harrison says, handing me a glass of iced tea.

"Let's have a seat."

We sit in the large wooden chairs, which are complete with nice, comfortable pillows. Taj and Dexter are comfortably lying at Harrison's feet. You can certainly see the loyalty the dogs have for their owner.

"So, tell me Mason. Why? Why does a young aspiring writer want to write about the likes of me?"

"Why? Your life has been extraordinary!"

"Good answer! Now, as I told you in my response letter – I am retired, therefore I don't work. That means you will have to do the work. I will enjoy sharing my stories and my life with you, but I won't do the work…"

"That is why I am here – sir, I mean Harrison"

"How long do you have Mason?"

"Six months to print!"

"Well, in six months, I'm going to take you through eight decades and we will be traveling. I don't spend more than two months in any one place, you know!"

"Yes, I have heard this about you."

"I don't like to get stagnant."

I knew after only the first two hours of meeting this man, that I was about to embark on a fascinating journey. He also made me aware of just how open he was about his life. He has no apologies and few regrets. Honestly, he reminds me of a monk. As we tour the home that looks as though it were torn out of a magazine, I couldn't help but compliment him on the style and décor.

"This is my dad's house. Everything about this house reflects him. Outdoors. No pretense. No façade, just quality and straightforwardness. This is where I come to be with my dad. My mom is reflected here as well, but it is dad's home."

"I noticed there are no photographs, Harrison."

"I do not like pictures – they underestimate and under-project the human experience. My photos are in my mind where they can only grow and not fade."

I must admit, I was a bit bummed. I expected to see volumes of photos from all over the world, and then I realized something as we continued our tour. Everything Harrison picked up had a story and he knew how to verbally take you on a visual journey. Harrison didn't have photos. He was able to put a movie projector in your mind and enable you to see the world through his words. He did this with complete ease and incredible detail – it was simply fascinating. The intensity with which he could describe the smallest of things was amazing and I realized then that my responsibility to this man and his story was an awesome one.

It was time to retire for the evening. The master bedroom was on the main floor and Harrison told me to make myself at home. He would see me in the morning. The boys seemed to beat Harrison to bed and I could hear Harrison say, "Scoot over!" Then I heard something that struck me as funny from this very commanding man. He pleaded with the boys by asking: "Please?" He was begging the boys earnestly to give him more room.

I slept remarkably well that evening. There was something very safe about this place – it was comforting. It seemed as though between these walls any subject could be confronted, any myth could be made real, and any stigma erased. That's why I came here.

Chapter 2

Into Town

When I awoke the next morning, I looked out of over the balcony windows off my bedroom. Harrison was wearing jeans, boots and a white pressed shirt and looked like an advertisement for Ralph Lauren. He sat, coffee in hand, gazing out over the river. He was intense and an extremely deep thinker. Not just deep, but also a concerned thinker – yet at peace with it all.

I knew from what I had read about this man, that he had experienced wonderful things in life. I also knew he had experienced horrific things. One couldn't help but see the burden he carried to this day. It seemed he carried it on his back; accepting the sincere responsibility he took in transforming it all into wisdom and inspiration. Harrison looked lonely as I watched him, but once again – he exuded peace. It was once written about Harrison that he was a living contradiction of himself – a walking oxymoron, if you will. I could see this complexity without even hearing his words.

The dogs were swimming in the river as I made my way downstairs. I see coffee is on the table with an empty traveler's mug. I pour myself a cup and head down the riverside path. The dogs both stop in the water and look straight at me and then to Harrison. I just knew I was about to be soaked by wet dogs when I heard a very demanding low voice say: **"Don't you dare!"**

The dogs turned and continued playing – Harrison turned and couldn't hold back his laughter.

"They are so very ornery!"

I too got the giggles. I was certain I was going to be attacked by the dogs with which Harrison always referred to as, 'the boys'.

"Good morning Mason, how did you sleep?"

"Like a baby, Harrison!"

"That is good to hear! I need to go into town this morning and make a trip to the market - would you like to join me?"

"Absolutely!"

"Good, let's fill our coffee cups and be on our way. You boys be good, we will go on the boat later this afternoon!"

I ask Harrison if he would like me to drive and he said: **"Yes, that would be nice – but we will take my car."**

We fill our coffee mugs and then go out a side door off the kitchen and head to the pole barn. Harrison presses a button and the garage door opens. He pushes another button and a car engine starts and he hands me the keys. As we turned the corner, I was surprised when I saw a four door black Bentley. I heard this guy had great taste.

"I've had this car for 25 years. I never knew how to take care of things when I was young and even middle-aged. In fact I was 45 years old when it hit me that I could actually keep something and be good to it. I love this car, but not for the car itself – but for the fact it is one of the first things I ever took care of."

"I'm a little nervous to drive such a nice car, Harrison."

"Don't be silly, it is just a car. I am just proud I didn't destroy it!"

I stepped into the Bentley and felt as giddy as the moment I had my first kiss. Sitting in the driver's seat of the Bentley, I experienced a rush- like I was doing something illegal. I had never felt such comfort in all my life and it was just a car! Harrison just smiles at my reaction.

"Some expenses justify themselves," he says with a wink.

Harrison slips on a pair of large dark sunglasses. He looks every bit the part of what I always imagined him to be – yet for Harrison, it is effortless, he just "is". We begin our drive down the wooded path.

As we drive down the road, my intensity begins to come into focus. I still can't stop thinking about how beautiful the leaves in Michigan are. It's almost as though the forest was a canvas, and the artist only had four colors to paint with. It seems as though the colors jump right out of the leaves! It's an amazing sight. But, before I can get so caught up in the beauty that I lose focus, Harrison makes an observation.

"Autumn is the time to fall in love. Spring is for romance and flings. Summer is for playing. But autumn – autumn is when man looks for someone to hibernate with during the winter and fall in love."

"Have you ever been in love Harrison?" I ask cautiously.

"Well of course – but no one ever loved me back! I never had luck with love. People could love one side of me but not the other and loving all of me is even a challenge for me. But falling in love is important to the human spirit. So, I did fall in love."

"And now, are you in love?"

"Oh, I love many. But I let go of the idea that partnership, romance or personal love would be a part of my life years and years ago. It was in my thirties that I gave up on that idea or illusion."

"That is awfully young to give up on love isn't it?"

"Maybe, but I knew it was going to take everything that I had to survive my own life and thereby thrive. One more disappointment in the 'love' department and I would be a goner! We will talk about those days at another time – it is too beautiful of a day to poison it with darkness."

When we arrived in town, Harrison asked me to park as far out as possible. "You miss so much when driving – I like to walk!"

Harrison is intense – I struggle to keep up as he hustles towards the market. But he's not rushing. His head moves all about as he notices all the color and detail. He looks at everything as if he had never seen it before. As we approached the fruit and vegetable market, his eyes become alive.

"I love this part" he says with a smile.

He waves to the vendors and they call out his name. Harrison handles each piece of produce with care and concern; much like a doctor with his patient. He fills his bag quite full. We leave the bag with one of the vendors and will pick it up on our way back to the car.

As we stroll through town, it is obvious that Harrison knows everyone, even some of the other townspeople. It is also obvious the distance he keeps with them. We stop into an upper crust pet supply store, where people can spoil their pets with the best of any product a pet would want or need. I immediately noticed items such as: toys, organic food, and treats. I am in awe to see the store clerk filling a basket while Harrison looks at the new toys. He finds one and with a silly, ornery smile says, **"Taj will love this but Dexter on the other hand will destroy it by next week!"**

The clerk says, "Will you bring the boys in before you head south?"

"Oh yes, we have a day planned so they can say their seasonal goodbyes. We will come by boat. They have a lot of people along the river to tend to, you know."

When I saw the total of the bill I thought to myself: 'I want to be Harrison's dogs!'

As we leave the shop, Harrison says, **"You know Mason, I was thinking this morning. Six months is really not going to be long enough. We would certainly be more relaxed and more productive over a full year. Do you think your publisher would extend your deadline?"**

"Actually, my editor, Frank, suggested one year. However, it was my understanding that six months was a long time to ask from you."

"Well, yes it is, but I like you – it is settled then, you will spend the year with me!"

I was elated. First that Harrison asked me to spend the year and secondly – within just 24 hours I felt as though I had undertaken an almost spiritual journey that I did not want to end.

It was a beautiful autumn day and warm enough to sit outside. We stopped for lunch at a corner café that provided a clear view of Lake Michigan from the patio seating. Harrison ordered a beer and Rueben. For no other reason than enjoying the moment, that sounded perfect to me as well.

"So far Harrison, I must say, I love your life!"

"Oh I have no doubt about that – I love my life as well!"

"Is this town about your dad as well?"

"I would say more mom, but dad loved town as well. Dad loved to be with mom so you could almost put him anywhere as long as she was there, except Macy's, that is! It is important realize that mom is the glue that has held our family together through experiences no family should ever have to go through."

"You miss your parents don't you?"

"I miss them unbearably. You will learn that I have very few regrets in my life Mason, one of them would be for every day I did not communicate with my parents. We can be so foolish at times. Our home here was built during the most horrific time in our lives and our home here would be responsible for mending those very wounds. A house was built here, but a home and a family were reinvented here."

"Your parents sound amazing!"

He laughed a hearty laugh from deep within: **"Ah, yes – look at me! Can you imagine raising me? I was my parent's only surviving child and I assure you I took the energy of a brood of six as I got older."**

"You had a sibling?"

Chuckling once again, Harrison said: **"Yes, my sister Athena. She would be 70 years old this past August – she would be OLD!"**

As the memory faded, I could hear Harrison's voice become somber and more serious: **"Athena died of a disease called Cystic Fibrosis. Anything that takes the life of a child must be cured – it is a horrible thing to lose a young life."** Harrison's eyes glazed over as he stared out over Lake Michigan. **"Well young man, we should be moving along."**

We pay our bill as Harrison says goodbye to all the familiar faces. So we begin to wander back, stopping at the butcher to pick out fresh meat and get the produce at the market. When we get into the car, Harrison says we have only one more stop out on the peninsula. He wants to buy two pounds of cherry beef jerky at a roadside vendor he obviously favored. Within an hour we make our way along the drive to the cabin.

"The boys are going to be wildly excited, just so you know!" Harrison says with a chuckle.

Sure enough as we emerge from the car – Taj and Dexter are wagging their tails so hard they can barely keep their balance. Making our way to the house Harrison places the boys' loot into what I learned is their refrigerator and hands Taj his new toy. Taj obviously knows what Harrison does and immediately disappears from Dexter. Dexter just likes to eat and Harrison hands him a rawhide bone. Dexter, happily satisfied with his new toy, flops down onto the floor.

With the boys happy, we start unloading the groceries. Harrison continues to inspect each piece of produce and meat.

"I love food! I'll make fresh salsa this afternoon and it'll be ready to enjoy tomorrow for lunch."

I retire to my room to write and make several calls. One call was to my editor, Frank, who is delighted to hear I will be devoting one year to Harrison Remy's life. After a couple of hours of work, I descend down the stairs to the smell of fresh vegetables and a kitchen filled with the aroma. Harrison is preparing his salsa.

The telephone rings and as Harrison hears the voice on the other end – he lights up with a huge smile.

"Olivia! And to what do I owe this grand occasion?" Olivia is Harrison's 2nd cousin and goddaughter. It is obvious he thinks the world of her as he is asking a million questions about her well-being. They seem to be talking about holiday plans.

"Yes, I will be on the farm the first of November, I will have a guest, Mason – he is writing about me, isn't that hilarious?" as Harrison laughs. **"No – you know I don't like to be a part of those individual soirée's, I will see you in November."** And they conclude their conversation. Harrison looks at me.

"I don't know what I would do if I had a large family – I can't keep track of the one I have!"

I ask Harrison if there is anything I can do to help but Harrison is very comfortable in his routine and doesn't want any interference. We head out to the back deck, where the boys are basking in the late afternoon sun.

Chapter 3

Coming Home

Harrison starts laughing: "I gave the boys a bit of a martini once. They are not good drinkers… They acted a fool and then passed out!" Harrison continues to talk.

"There are many memories here. My parents and I spent all of July here every year. I can't bear to be here in July now; I only spend the autumn here. Summers are in the city. My mother enjoyed reading here and dad fishing. I generally wrote. It was difficult trying to keep my parents still for any length of time. They always had to keep busy. The first time I came here, I was 37 years old. I had not spent quality time with my parents for nearly 10 years. The darkest years of our lives were those 10 years. When we arrived that July, we had become a family transformed. I was weak, completely beaten up by life at that point. I was also surprised that I had even survived the past 10 years. I was exhausted on every level and my parents realized this and gave me the time and nurturing of emotions that my soul craved. Those years seem unreal, but the lasting effect has been very real."

"Harrison, it's been 43 years since the end of what you call the 'dark years' and I can see, in your face the effects are as if it were yesterday."

"Human beings are animals, Mason – make no mistake about it. Just like a rat being backed into a corner, they will attack you with all their might and aim to kill. Now mind you, I love human beings, I love people. But I never underestimate a

person's ability to be very dangerous. We all have it and we as human beings, if unable to communicate the emotions we feel, get backed into that proverbial corner. We all have the ability to be very ugly. No human is without this flaw. As psychology has advanced and continues to do so, the science gradually gets proven.

Today, you can step into a machine and see deficiencies, chemical or otherwise. These are treated medically now rather than mentally. I never liked taking my medications. Every time I saw them, I thought to myself, "You are deficient, a mistake – not whole, not normal but different in a bad way. To know that raging demons that are liars and chameleons live inside of you is a terrible thing. A cross I wish no one to bear."

Chapter 4

Mental Illness

"Can we talk about your mental illness, Harrison?"

"Of course – it is as much a part of me as my blue eyes. I both love it and hate it, but am always terrified of it. Most people have an angel on one shoulder and the devil on the other. But some of us have an army of demons on one shoulder and on the other, an army of angels. Most don't need to concern themselves with the ongoing battle of wrong or right. It is instinctually and the decision process is a millisecond long. Some however go through a grueling process of not right or wrong – but what is real and what is not. For 28 years of my life I knew I was tormented. I had no idea by what and I certainly did not know to what extent. My reality was very distorted, very confused. To this day, I deal with emotions that are real but I am not always sure if what causes those emotions is real or not."

I asked Harrison: "If you had known how the madness tormented you, how would things have been different?"

With very intent, ice blue eyes, Harrison looked at me.

"Speculation on one's self and on others is a dangerous and damning game. I don't play games!"

I learned my first very important lesson about Harrison – he doesn't take the words 'should have, would have or could have' lightly. In fact he takes them very seriously.

"I think I will throw some Black and Blue Hamburgers on the grill and cut fresh potatoes for frying – does that sound good, Mason?"

"Does it ever!"

Harrison first fires up the grill, and we step back inside where he cuts chunks of blue cheese from a big wheel and mixes it with seasoning into the ground sirloin. Setting the bowl in the refrigerator, he pulls out a basket of potatoes – cleans them and begins to hand slice French fries. Turning on the burner on the grill, he sets a large pot of oil onto it. What I thought sounded like a daunting task for dinner was done effortlessly in 20 minutes!

Dinner is incredible; like a gourmet American meal the finest hotel would prepare and charge a fortune for. After dinner, Harrison pours us each a glass of Cabernet. "Let's sit in the kitchen, Mason, the best things happen in the kitchen."

What becomes obvious to me is that Harrison takes the complexity out of life. He somehow views everything as a series of motions rather than an overall project that often times finds us to be stagnating.

"When I was thirteen years old my dad and his friend Daryl bought a soft serve ice cream machine. I never knew what came over them to do so, but they did. That Halloween they set it up at the general store in town and handed out ice cream cones to local kids who were trick-or-treating. They then proceeded to convert an old meat locker into an ice cream parlor called the "Double Dip".

Daryl and my dad often did small and fun business ventures together. My dad was not a gambling man nor did he venture outside of reality very often. Yet he had the best

instincts I have ever known. He was generally the only one that wouldn't trust those instincts. Ironically, he was so well respected that if he told someone to jump off a bridge, they most generally would. Dad was simply himself in any situation.

For five years, every summer, the "Double Dip" became a place of employment for me, my cousins, and my friends. Yes, we had our little spats, but for the most part we all worked very well together. One or two years, I even ran the little business. Silently and humbly my dad had provided not only for myself, but for all of us. That is where he was most comfortable, doing something good for others – but silently."

The sun was setting over the horizon, ushering in the end of the day. The home was even more spectacular from behind. Spotlights lit up the entire yard and dock. Once again it was time to retire for the evening and yet another productive and inspiring day with Harrison Remy was over.

Chapter 5

A Day with Harrison

PULL – BANG – PULL – BANG! What the hell? I am awakened by gun shots and what sounded like four men having a shooting party. I looked out over the balcony and there was only one man at this party- it was Harrison. Singlehandedly he was pulling the pigeon launcher and shooting. I make my way down stairs, grab a cup of coffee and head out.

"That looks a little complicated, Harrison!"

Harrison grins and then says: **"You learned to become very resourceful when you are an only child, Mason!"**

"Are you practicing for the hunting season?"

"Oh no, I don't hunt – that was my dad's thing. Actually I saw Ms. Elson pull in last night across the river – I thought I would welcome her pretentious ass up north!"

A very ornery look comes across Harrison's face.

"I love to drive her wild and that is my objective for today!"

Harrison had seemed to find some joy in a place that I had never expected him to find joy.

Ms. Elson was a wealthy woman and as I later found out a very bitter conservative woman that thought that not only were Harrison's causes useless, but ridiculous. Rather than argue with her, Harrison would simply heighten his eccentricity to an irritating level.

I would later learn that when confronted with stereotyping and stigma, Harrison would often exaggerate himself in order to put push the point across what he called the "Archie Bunker" mentality.

Chapter 6

Harrison's Routine

"Today is a busy day. I have a young lady who comes on Wednesdays to help me clean and organize as well as help me with some administrative stuff," Harrison says.

"I've noticed that your home is immaculate!"

"My life has to be extremely organized – everything around me must be in its place or my mind falls into chaos. It is a prevention thing, really – the organizing that is. I am not really that anal retentive, it just happens that I must be in order to keep my mind from shutting down. It is important to know just how serious I take my mental illness, Mason. I am 80- years old and still have a trustee write my checks. There is a very simple, but large system around me and my finances."

"Does that burden you?"

"No, not at all. These things have been very disruptive in the past; people and family who care about me have put systems in place to protect me from myself or my illness."

In the distance, I hear the front door shut, and the sound of a young female voice holler: "Hello."

"AH – Ruthie is here!"

Ruthie enters the room, and she appears to be about 30 years old, with red hair and a truly pale, Irish complexion. She's not what most people would consider to be enormously attractive. But she has a remarkable plainness to her face, in such a way that it seems to be uncommonly common. She walks out to the porch. She has boxes and bags full of stuff. Harrison looks at me and laughs.

"I refuse to go to a Wal-Mart. My cousin, Lydia told me they have subliminal messages making you spend more money than you want to – I have enough voices in my head, so I send Ruthie instead!" Harrison exclaims and then laughs hysterically.

"You hardly strike me as a person that believes such a thing, Harrison!"

"Actually, you are right –however, my cousin Lydia is generally right about everything so I don't take a chance!"

As I look at all the packages and boxes Ruthie hauls into the house, I start to believe if there are subliminal messages – and Ruthie is not immune to them. There are paper towels by the box, tooth paste, and large quantities of every other household nick-knack. Noticing my facial expression Harrison says:

"By the way – this is a once a year thing."

While Harrison is busy unpacking the boxes, Ruthie is gathering her cleaning supplies. Harrison introduces Ruthie to me. I am pleased to meet such a caring person who is almost motherly towards Harrison.

"We need to get the boys fattened up for their trip, Ruthie," Harrison says with a smile.

"Their trip?" I ask

"Yes, the boys go to Ohio for two months only and then they fly to South Africa a month before I follow, as they have to be quarantined for 30 days per South African law. It works out okay, as they are too rambunctious for the holidays. While it pains me to quarantine them – it would be worse to leave them for two or three months."

"These are some world traveling pups!" I say as I bend down and pet them behind their ears.

"Oh yes, they have more friends throughout the world than I have. They don't know a stranger, unfortunately... On the South African plantation those strangers include zebra, wildebeest, wild boar and God knows what else. They are never allowed unescorted on the plantation or in the bush. At times it can be worrisome but we have, at great cost, made the provisions for them. You will see when you get there. By the way, Ruthie, there are some papers and mail in my office you need to tend to."

Ruthie hands Harrison a banking envelope full of cash.

"Oh great! My allowance!"

"Allowance?" I ask, somewhat surprised.

Ruthie speaks right up, "You can hand him a hundred dollars a day and he will spend it or you can hand him ten thousand dollars a day and he will spend it – to this day, I have no idea on what!"

"Blah Blah Blah," Harrison laughs as he counts his money.

"Well, Mason – we need to get out of the house or we'll be kicked out by Ruthie – since I have some money, let's go boating!" Harrison says ecstatically.

In a loving, but authoritative voice, Ruthie says, "YOU are washing the car and organizing the pole barn."

"I have the only illness in the world that requires me to pay someone to boss me around!" Harrison says rolling his eyes.

We head out the front door towards the pole barn. I offer to wash the car while Harrison organizes. I don't understand what he needs to organize. Everything looks perfect. I hear the stereo being turned up with fun 80's and 90's hits and have to laugh as this 80 year old man is singing along to Madonna.

Chapter 7

A Glimpse into Harrison's Past

After an hour of cleaning the car and perfecting the pole barn, Harrison says it's time for lunch. We head inside. Ruthie is upstairs; I hear the laundry going and the vacuum.

"She is a machine!" Harrison laughs.

Harrison takes out the salsa he made yesterday along with tortilla chips and colds cuts with Rye Bread. There must have been 20 different mustards and different flavored mayonnaise and dressings. "It is my dad's house, but mom's refrigerator and she loved condiments!"

"Have you been to Mexico City, Mason?"

"No, I haven't."

"I love Mexico City. It is complete chaos which matches my chaotic mind!

One long weekend, I flew to Mexico City to meet my friends, Daniel and Ari. Daniel's an executive with a motion picture company. Ari's a book translator. Daniel was an east coast trust fund brat and Ari, a Jewish immigrant to Mexico. They were pieces of work, those two. Marrisa was our mutual friend and the head of the Four Seasons in Mexico City. Mind you – I was most likely out of my mind during those times.

I knew Daniel from the LA days and missed seeing him. They invited me for the weekend so I went. It could have

been a very normal trip – however, nothing in my life is generally normal. It always intrigued me, looking back at how I put myself in some very interesting positions. I always asked to be upgraded to first class and 90 percent of the time, I was. Arriving in Mexico City when you are a guest of the Four Seasons and flying first class, customs is somewhat a luxurious adventure rather than a combination of lines and frustration. At least it was then.

Arriving, I was guided to a separate area where I was processed into the country. From there I was taken to a private car and whisked away to the Four Seasons. I doubt those I was traveling with were even through customs by the time I arrived at the hotel. Admittedly, I enjoyed this celebrity treatment."

As Harrison starts to tell of this time, you can see the excitement in his eyes. Harrison's dad once said of Harrison: "Putting him in the city is like putting a kid in a candy shop!" I could definitely see how Harrison's energy was building just reminiscing about the energy of Mexico City. Listening to Harrison discuss his time in Mexico City with friends made me realize, once again, just how small the world really is to Harrison.

What Harrison was not able to do was put a timeline together of the trip. He remembered some specific events and some conversations, but he couldn't remember in what order they occurred. That troubled him as he tried to put it all together as he spoke.

It is amazing the lengths the subconscious will go to keep you from yourself, especially in a troubled mind. I took a walk along the river while Harrison took a nap. I continued to ask myself what those days were like when Harrison and his parents would spend their July's here in Michigan. He had mentioned the amount of visitors they would have in any given week. They must have had a very good time and I was eager to learn more. Although now, it seemed Harrison didn't have many visitors.

As I approached the steps to the porch, Ruthie emerged from the house.

"Are you enjoying your stay, Mason?"

"I am indeed. He's truly intriguing!"

"Yes that he is. Harrison is his own unique person."

"How long have you worked for Harrison?"

"I've helped out around here for about 10 years. Harrison is incredibly generous. He paid for my education."

"What's your degree in?"

"Art History. I told Harrison I had no real use for a college degree as I had no aspirations of leaving here or changing my life. I'm very content here. Harrison's reply was: 'What does gaining knowledge have to do with leaving your life? What is something you are interested in learning?'"

"I just said, 'I love art,' to which he replied, 'then you will go to college and learn about art!' He has his beliefs, and liked to make them known. He was adamant that I get an education. So I did. The day I left for my freshman year, he told me: 'This country has a disease that believes we were born to be a part of a machine – that higher education is for the betterment of that machine – higher education is for the betterment of you – screw the machine! There are plenty of people who want to be a part of the machine – so let them be just that!'"

"So, I went to school and thoroughly enjoyed learning about art and its history. Now Harrison would tell you that he sent me to school so that I could teach him about art history. In a way I did. Whenever I came to the house on a break or to help him, I would sit for hours and tell Harrison what I had learned. However, it was Harrison that would bring art and its history to life. He would take me on a verbal journey through the most incredible museums of the world."

"That is amazing!"

"He is an amazing person, Mason. He's the happiest man I have ever met and also the saddest." She said as she bowed her head, lowered her voice and turned back to the house.

Once again, there was that very definition that spoke of his contradiction. I sat for a while making notes. As I was finishing up, Harrison and the boys stepped onto the porch.

Chapter 8

The Boat Ride

"Mason, my man! How are you? Do you have a chapter completed?" as he laughed.

"I have some notes for a few chapters actually . Would you like to review?"

"Oh heavens no, I spent 37 years of my life caring what people thought of me and I still care what the people of that 37 years think or thought, but no one after that. I put a stop to that self-destruction 37 years too late. Where is Ruthie?"

Ruthie was not far behind. She shouted to Harrison as she walked towards the porch: "Right here!"

"You are staying for dinner, right?"

"Sure! What are we having?"

"Mexican chicken!"

It is nearly four in the afternoon. Harrison decided that we all need to take a boat ride. The boys heard the word "boat" and were already aboard waiting anxiously. We made our way down to the boat and loaded up. Harrison has a cooler this time. He said, "Happy hour will be a beer or two for each on the boat!"

It is a beautiful, crisp, late afternoon. Sweatshirts are enough to keep us comfortable. We slowly start around the perimeter of the river and float downstream. There are only a few homes on the river as we head towards the adjacent lake. The lake is 1,200 acres surrounded by national forest and no homes – just nature. Ruthie and Harrison recap old stories of cruising the lake and the "fish stories" that come along with any lake.

Harrison asks me about my family:

"My dad is in Milwaukee, my mom in Chicago." I wasn't interested in getting to the details of my life and I guess that Harrison picked up on that as he asked no further questions. After about an hour of cruising, Harrison breaks open the cooler and offers everyone a beer. The boys seem to be eager for one as well, but Harrison lectures them on their drinking behavior and they go back to the head of the boat as if they are guiding the boat themselves.

As the sun begins to set, Harrison is making his way back up the river. He says, "Anyone up for McLaughlin's Pub?" I've heard of many places that Harrison likes to go, but not this place. Without hesitation, Ruthie says: "That sounds fun!"

So before long, we dock, and Harrison makes a call. Someone from the pub will drive down to the river and pick us up. Sure enough, by the time we were on land, a Jeep pulls down the hill and a chipper man by the name of Jay jumps out, and welcomes us: "Harrison, nice to see you!" Jay says, offering Harrison his hand. Harrison grabs his hand and brings Jay's body close enough for a bear hug. Harrison and Jay make small talk along our way to the pub. The boys seemed comfortable, as they lay down in the back.

As we walk in, the boys seem to be very familiar with the routine. Not even two miles up the road is a public house in the old world style, very authentic, yet very stylish; not just some corner bar with a folksy Irish name. This was a true Irish Pub.

The doors open, and sure enough, the boys are the first to enter. It's funny to me; the boys act as though this is their bar, and the doors opened just for them. It seems McLaughlin's is aware of the boys' drinking behavior, as the boys have a beer in their bowl before we have one in our hands!

Harrison chuckles to us as he takes his first swig: "I love the Irish, you always feel sober around them!"

Harrison starts working the room. He seems to know everyone in the pub and engages in small talk, not ignoring anyone. Ruthie and I park ourselves on a bar stool. It is interesting to watch Harrison interact with people. He's very social but very reserved as well. Even though he seems to be the center of attention he is more of an observer than a focal point. While it seems from afar that the all the regulars are there for him, from his demeanor you can tell that it is the other way around. Harrison is there for them. He snakes through the crowd and returns to where Ruthie and I are seated.

"Have you been to Ireland my boy?"

"No, I haven't."

"It's a beautiful country with loyal, friendly people! My grandmother was Irish. She either liked you or didn't – no gray areas, no bullshit either! You were well aware if she didn't like you and I admire that in the Irish – no bullshit. My grandmother was one of my favorite people in the world. And I, hers. Grandma loved her family and did all she could to make sure *her* family had a family that she really didn't have."

I could see a glaze coming over Harrison's eyes. When Harrison felt – he felt deeply and it was always visible. Ruthie pats Harrison on the back,

"I'll never forget the story about the dishes, Harrison!" Harrison smiles as Ruthie continues, "Imagine Harrison as a little boy, around five or six. He sat at the dining room table at his grandma's house and bellowed orders to his grandma while she did the dishes. He'd yell; 'I want this, I want that, I want to do this, I want to do that.' His grandmother – not one for spoiled brats, slammed the dishes down, turned around with soap on her hands and yelled: 'Harrison, you don't always get what you want!'" His grandmother then observed the most honestly shocked look that came across Harrison's face. She then realized, 'Oh my – no one has ever told him that before!' Harrison's face showed complete horror to this new found information. She dried off her hands and then looked at Harrison and said, 'Well, okay – you can have what you want but you have to wait until the dishes are done!'

We all broke out into laughter. Harrison too, though through tears running down his cheeks, once again showing this amazing contradiction in Harrison. This man could both laugh and cry genuinely at the same time. **"No one ever made me feel as protected and as important as my grandma."** Silence followed the laughter, as the tears continued to flow from Harrison's eyes. Ruthie patted his back again, "And thank God for her, because she taught you to do the same for SO many!"

Harrison wiped his tears away along with the moment and rounded us up to get back to the boat. We made our way back to the cabin and all met in the kitchen, while Harrison finished making dinner. Throughout dinner, Ruthie and Harrison engage in conversation about Spanish architecture and Aztec pottery. The knowledge of this man was amazing, but not academic. His knowledge came from what he had seen and experienced in life and obviously absorbed so deeply.

As always, with Harrison, I could tell that while he reminisces, he also had that hidden sadness in the back of his eyes. His blue eyes radiate that latent sadness and the overall depth he carried with him. It was almost as though there was a secret, that I never saw going through the archives about him. It was almost as though he knew something that he wasn't telling. The question intrigued me, and I was determined to find out what that secret was. It was abundantly clear that that secret held the key to the man; a man that I most desperately wanted to unlock.

That evening I retired to my room early to reflect on the past few days and review my research on Harrison. Harrison was born into what most would call a very normal, hardworking, middle class family. However, Harrison was everything but a reflection of normality. I already knew he had lived a controversial life as well as a difficult one at times. What most had said about him was the fact that he had an amazing resilience and insight into his own experiences. Obviously, he was resilient, but there was much more to it than just bouncing back after tribulations. One of the more important things that I noticed about Harrison is while he may have physically and mentally been able to overcome extraordinary circumstances – emotionally, he was very close to those experiences. I found it difficult to sleep that night.

Chapter 9

The Early Years

The following dawn was beautiful. As I looked out over the lake I could see the mist that hung near the water refracting the morning sun, in a way that made me feel at peace, a peace that I so rarely feel. When I went downstairs Harrison asked if I wanted to go boating. It isn't even a question in my mind. Soon we untie the boat, and we set sail. We decided to simply hang out on the boat, floating on the peaceful water. In my mind, I thought this was the perfect opportunity to get to know Harrison a little more.

"Harrison, what was the most difficult time in your life?"

"There is not a single time that was the most difficult; it was a collection of times – most were a reflection of an illness I was not even aware of. I was given everything in my young life. Yes, there was the death of my sister and in the beginning we didn't have a lot, but we always had what we needed. My parents and everyone around me were busy taking care of those needs.

I was an only child and while I never really lacked for attention – I was alone in my thoughts a lot and I thought a lot more than maybe I wished I did. Often times, when I discuss my childhood, it comes across as if it was sad and that really wasn't the case. My mind was sad. My environment was wonderful and completely normal – it was my mind and emotions that were quite different. I always knew there was a difference but I was not sure how I was to articulate that or if

I should. Early on, I realized that most around me were normal and did not think like me. At a young age, I didn't know if that was bad or good.

I spent countless hours as a child writing and throwing away what I wrote. I spent many nights in tears wanting to be normal. I prayed a lot and at times even before my teens, decided God just didn't like me. When I was a little boy I thought, if God doesn't like you, then it would be pretty difficult for anyone else to like you as well, right?

Those times definitely started what I would call my acting career!"

"You were an actor?"

Laughing, "No, not in the professional sense – but in my own life. Somehow, I was going to find a way to be accepted and through my teen years, I worked very hard at finding just how I was going to do that.

I watched people closely – I emulated people at times. When you are a teenager, you don't exactly think clearly anyway – but when you are a teenager that has convinced yourself that even some of your family, don't 'like' you or who you are – you will go to some pretty extreme levels to be liked or at least get the attention you crave.

Many people throughout my life would most likely say this is untrue. Untrue, just like many things people have said through the years. It really doesn't matter if it was true or not, if I felt it, it was true to me. Self-righteous people have an amazing way of making you feel that you are not seeing the truth even when you are and then convincing you that you are the liar. When you are young and you haven't experienced much in life and you grow up in a small town, a small world – you can only believe what they say and look at yourself as a fool.

I got through those years and I did it the best I knew how. I had many so called friends and I was, in my opinion, always thought of as a nice guy. My high school years were even fun at times – but it was an act that I could have received an academy award for.

Unfortunately I missed one step as I was entering adulthood. I missed it because everyone around me only saw the character that I had developed and I realized that in order to actually ask for advice in my life – I would have to reveal myself. I wasn't willing to take that chance so I missed that step. I missed a great learning opportunity and I had lost sight of myself. Much of that was contributed to a bipolar mind. The illness strengthens throughout the years."

"So all those people who were friends and family through your first, say eighteen years, didn't know the real you?"

"No, they didn't or they didn't know the complete me. They saw what I wanted them to see. They saw the character that I developed that I knew would be well received – they never saw me.

Family and friends never saw the countless nights of tears, the letters written and thrown away; the emotional roller coaster of gigantic proportions; and the demons that I wrote off as "adolescence" were never visible to anyone but me. I confided in one person, and she wasn't even alive. I confided in my dead sister Athena. My grandmother had a sixth sense about it all as well."

"Would you consider that hallucinating?"

"No, Athena was never a hallucination; she was a reality that I kept alive to keep me alive. I guess some might say I was losing it then, had they known – but I needed a friend, a confidant and someone that wasn't going to turn their back in laughter or hatred and Athena couldn't do that! I knew that and that is why it was not a hallucination. I knew Athena was dead, but she was my resource for divine advice because I believed that God only liked children like my cousins, Lydia, Dan and Demi. It is important to realize that this is a part of the illness of bipolar disorder. Had I not grown up in such a stable environment where I was allowed the freedom and safety that I had, my life would have been much different and I would have been in huge trouble, I have no doubt about that!"

"Harrison, it's so sad that you grew up in that silence and pain. Can you elaborate on that?"

"Well, Mason, I also grew up in a beautiful home, with a beautiful family; with money, friends, and opportunity. I was not abused by anyone; I was encouraged by my parents. I didn't know that there was an entity living inside my mind slowly and patiently gaining power and control over my life. No one else did either. How could they?"

I sat and stared at the water and tree line for what seemed like hours. The thoughts of a young man being tormented and convinced by what was not necessarily reality really bothered me. I knew that Harrison grew up in a small town, where minds can be narrow and diversity was not wildly accepted. Here was a kid that was fighting to make damn sure he appeared normal. While Harrison said that it was no one's fault, I struggled with that mindset. I didn't feel that it was his parents fault but that it was a fault of society as a whole. Why is it that in our society, we mourn the cancer victim, but scorn a person with a mental illness? It almost seemed that as Harrison spoke of his struggles with identity and youth, that this could be the secret that he kept within himself. Was this the secret that he was hiding? Did it have to do with the façade, the act? Or was it something greater? I turned away from the water, and looked at him. I had to ask:

"Harrison, when was your first thought of suicide?"

Harrison slowly looked up at me and a tear dropped from his right eye.

"Thirteen, I was thirteen. A math teacher humiliated me in the 7th grade in front of a class of many people I did not know. He set the bar for the perception my peers would have. It was the first time in my life that I learned a human being could be cold. It was also the validation that I needed to realize I could not be whoever I really was – that was not going to be acceptable to all around me."

Harrison's eyes immediately drifted off to look across the water.

"What would you say to that thirteen year old now?"

Harrison's head snapped back to look at me.

"I would say, 'you haven't seen anything yet kid!'"

I was somewhat shocked by his answer.

"Wouldn't you give him any advice to change the path and nurture his emotions?"

"To another kid, yes, but not to me. I would not change a thing, I can't change a thing and the reality is the level of coldness that that teacher expressed doesn't begin to touch the surface of what I would later experience in life. It was good I learned that people could hate or at least be hateful."

"What kept you from attempting suicide?"

"I went home to safety. I went home to stability. I never went home to chaos and hatred – had I not lived in that environment, life would have been different if it existed at all. I was fortunate. I'm not saying that those kids who do follow through with suicide are less fortunate – I'm simply saying that I was fortunate all the way around. I'm not one to throw a lot of blame around, however – a teacher or even a peer that finds any satisfaction at all in demeaning and humiliating another person or child is very dangerous. Very dangerous, indeed!"

Harrison and I spent the next few hours out on the water and turned the conversation to more positive subjects like changing leaves and the clear water. I was starting to learn when to push and when to step back when it came to Harrison's past.

Chapter 10

Oliver

In all the time I'd been around Harrison, I'd never seen him get upset. Today, he got a call that clearly upset him. It was the first time I saw him have those feelings. With a heavy heart he sighed:

"My friend Oliver needs me. He's at his cabin about an hour from here."

Harrison pours a cup of coffee for each of us.

"I will give you some history. I met Oliver when he was 24 and I was 36. We were in a county lock up together. He was in for using drugs. Oliver was heavily addicted to heroin and cocaine. So much so, the night he was arrested he was being resuscitated after having had a heart attack from mixing the two. He had enough illegal drugs in his possession to be sent to prison. Oliver was extremely intelligent and also dealt with bipolar disorder. His mother, a German; and his father, a Caledonian made a very good looking and intelligent young man. I sort of adopted the young guy as my son at the time. It frustrated me that drugs were destroying him. His mother even began writing me in jail because she noticed a change in her son after the two of us met.

I kept in touch with Oliver over the years. He had aspirations of being a writer and a lyricist. He achieved both with great success. He was engaged prior to prison to a girl named Beatrice. After his release they reunited and married.

Forty years later, Beatrice left him. He is now alone and simply a mess. Beatrice didn't make it easy. She tried and nearly succeeded to take him for all he had.

His two sons and I stood up for Oliver and his mental state during his relapse to ensure she didn't finish him off financially or mentally. She had no reasonable excuse to leave Oliver – just that she was done. Beatrice was given a reasonable and very comfortable settlement; however, she had gone for blood and she nearly got just that – Oliver's blood.

When Oliver called this morning, he stated that "it" is simply unbearable. I translate that as a suicidal risk and I must go!"

"Of course!"

It was obvious that Harrison was very upset and fortunately Ruthie spent the night. She could take care of a few personal things for Harrison. As Harrison and I are walking out, Ruthie looks at me and says, "I have a strange feeling about this!"

After an hour drive and dead silence, Harrison and I step into Oliver's home. Oliver's cabin was a cabin that made Harrison's cabin look like a guest house. Oliver had made an incredible success of himself first through the medium of magazine articles and then as a correspondent, writer and lyricist. He then went on to write bestselling novels. The house was a reflection of this success, a sprawling log cabin that certainly registered as a mansion.

Harrison was unimpressed and knew exactly where to find Oliver. We headed straight up the stairs, made a right into what looked like another entry way to another home, but was actually just a master suite the size of most homes – I gasped. Harrison turned and looked at me, saying: "Mania and money! This is the definition of it!"

There, sitting on a large leather sofa was Oliver wearing a robe and looking completely disheveled.

"Oliver, old chap! What can I do? Name it! Name it and consider it done!"

"My housekeeper, Genevieve called Shelly this morning." Oliver says.

"Okay." Harrison says with obvious concern.

Shelly was pleasant enough, however her blood, pumped from her heart, didn't contain one vessel of compassion. Just the mention of her name, seemed to ignite a fire in Harrison's eyes-the fire of rage. She had always made Oliver feel guilt and sorrowful remorse. She did this in spite of the fact that Oliver provided a great deal of luxury for her and her family. Shelly always believed Oliver's "problems" caused her to lose out on the best years of her life. Harrison was never real impressed with Shelly's manipulation but generally kept his mouth shut about it.

As Harrison turned and looked on the coffee table, he literally stepped back and gasped. What he saw on the table was cocaine! He looked at Oliver. Tears streaming down his old friend's face, Oliver said, "Harrison, what have I done?"

Harrison grabbed his dear friend and held him tight.

"You haven't done anything, Oliver. The madness attacked you when you were weak!"

"Harrison, I drove to Detroit, by myself. I drove into the city, in a Rolls Royce, by myself. I bought cocaine from a kid on the street – just like I did 40 years ago. He wanted 120 bucks; I gave him a stack of hundred dollar bills and drove all the way back up north."

Harrison lunges forward… **"My God, I am so thankful we still have you!"**

I must admit, while standing there, looking around at this incredible home, knowing the success of Oliver and all that he had accomplished and all he knew Harrison would do for him, I was a little aggravated. I'm not sure, but if I had been Harrison, I would have slapped Oliver – not hugged him! I was about to see a lesson in life and a lesson amongst men.

"Forty years Harrison, forty damn years and I go straight for an eight ball of coke!"

"What are you lithium levels, Oliver?"

"I haven't checked in a week!"

Harrison jumped to his feet.

"Well, we have many things to do this year. There is South Africa, you in Paris – so let's get this shit under control. YOU, Oliver – do nothing. Just don't argue with me, okay?"

"I'm sorry Harrison." Oliver said in a broken voice.

"Don't you ever say that to me again!" Harrison said, as he fought back tears.

"Geneviève!" Harrison screamed then looked at me, **"The size of this house is ridiculous!"** Geneviève arrives.

"Geneviève, my dear – please get rid of that cocaine, run a hot bath, and get the most comfortable pajamas Oliver has!"

"Can I do anything for you Mr. Remy" Geneviève says in concern.

"No, my dear – I am heading to the kitchen to make macaroni and cheese!"

Geneviève got a strange look on her face, as did I.

"WELL – you have to have comfort food at time like this! One more thing – see what "feel good movies" you can find in that monstrosity of a theatre Oliver has! I will find all the comfort food in the house, close the blinds, bring the movies up here. Today is a comfy and safe day! In fact, get us all pajamas."

Harrison shows a grin, but as he walks by me – all emotion went out of his face when I heard him whisper – **"I hate this damn disease!"**

I met up with Harrison in the kitchen where he didn't say much but was visibly irate. Not at Oliver, but at this unseen illness that has taken the lives of so many he knows and destroyed the lives of others. It is as if you can see all the faces of the past flashing through Harrison's eyes on an endless loop..

Harrison prepared the most incredible smoked Gouda mac and cheese I have ever seen. Obviously I was in a different tax bracket here, because I don't keep smoked Gouda on hand in my tiny apartment in Chicago!

Harrison then reached for the phone and pushes one button.

"Dr. Ebel? Harrison Remy here!" Dr. Ebel is a psychiatrist at the Mayo Clinic in Rochester, MN. He's Harrison's psychiatrist as well as Oliver's. Harrison told Dr. Ebel of the recent events and he makes plans for tomorrow.

After an hour or so and a lot of silence, Shelly bursts through the kitchen door and screams for Geneviève in an indignant tone:. Harrison snaps off the kitchen bar stool and Shelly is a bit shocked to see Harrison standing there.

Harrison has always had an incredible way with words. A silver sword tongue, he has been called more than once. He could give you a warm hug with his words or he could slice you in half.

"Shelly, nice to see you – I see you are 'filling out' just like your mother!" Harrison says with clear intent.

Shelly most likely had no less than ten plastic surgeries in her life and seemed more like a medusa than a temptress. With just a few words, Harrison made very clear that Shelly's dramatics were going to stop.

"Your brother is taking a bath and cleaning up. He's had a hard couple of days. Why don't you go on up and say hello," he says as Shelly remains quiet and respectful. She ascends the stairs to Oliver's room.

Oliver is now in his pajamas, exhausted, but still a bit anxious from the cocaine. Shelly simply says, "Hello Oliver". Harrison enters the room and asks everyone to sit down. Harrison explains, in brief, what has happened and the plans he has made. Shelly, it seems, is never short on drama. She bursts into tears and hysterical behavior. I've never been sure if the hysterics are real; or if it's just drama, but Harrison seems intent on overcoming the many failings of the evening. But before he can say the healing words I expect him to say, Shelly has an outburst:

"HOW COULD YOU! You have disappointed me just like you have all your life. COCAINE, MY GOD OLIVER you are an OLD MAN! Once a junkie, always a junkie!"

Harrison rose to feet and seemed to keep rising like a lion about to attack. His shoulders seem to expand as though he was a king cobra and his eyes became fiercely blue.

"I say", he says, with a deep voice that I had not heard from Harrison. **"You ungrateful, spoiled, uncompassionate ingrate! Your tears are not that for Oliver, but for YOU! Your selfishness has been the ugliness that has plagued you your whole life Shelly and YOU WILL NOT inflict more pain on my friend any longer. Take your shallow mind, your pathetic snobbery and get the hell out of this house – AT ONCE! Someone will call you with updates on Oliver's condition. I, on the other hand never want to see your face again – get out of my sight!"**

Shelly, quickly leaves with no comment. The air becomes heavy, and it feels hot if only for a moment. She knew her manipulation was at an end, much like a salmon knows it will die after swimming upriver to spawn. She was seething with jealousy that Oliver had such a devoted friend.

Geneviève is visibly shaken and intimidated. Harrison puts his arm around her and says, **"Thank you for being a wonderful lady and a wonderful person to Oliver for so many years,"** he says as she turns and uses Harrison's shoulder as a safe place to cry. Then a voice comes from the sofa – "I've wanted to tell that bitch off for forty years!" said Oliver in a very dry tone and we all started laughing hysterically.

Harrison starts serving mac and cheese and insists that Geneviève make herself comfortable, as we all watch a movie. The movie begins and plays on to our mild amusement. It was a somber amusement, as Oliver had just relapsed, but still, I felt as though we were well taken care of. I don't know if it was the fact that we were eating expensive macaroni and cheese, or if we were just on edge because of the shortcomings of the night; but I felt tired. Judging by the droopiness of Harrison's eyes I felt we all did. Sure enough, everyone fell asleep and didn't wake up until morning.

I thought the next morning might be a bit awkward; however, it wasn't. Oliver came into the kitchen, then Harrison. Harrison had a few telephone calls to make and Oliver introduced himself to me. Today, Oliver looked every bit the part of the success he really was. He laughed a little about the fact that I was writing about 'that old fart'. Harrison and Oliver decided to take a morning walk with their coffee and I stayed behind in the kitchen, simply collecting my thoughts of all that had happened the day before.

Shelly's words really bothered me, however my first instinct when I saw Oliver, was indeed to slap him. It continuously crossed my mind how things would be different had Harrison not been there. What would have happened to Oliver?

Oliver had not used drugs in forty years; he was willing to risk his life to escape whatever emotional and mental pain he was in. Was he risking his life to tempt the fates? Was he trying to die? Did I just meet someone that wanted to die?

Harrison's reaction was somewhat surprising as well. I am not sure I ever saw a person so livid and protective at the same time; yet, compassionate and heartfelt. Was Harrison speaking on behalf of just Oliver or was he speaking to more than just Shelly and on behalf of himself? The emotion was deep and the reaction that Shelly had given obviously sparked something inside of Harrison that he had felt before.

My mind wandered in all different directions. If a person doesn't have that sense of decorum or the ability to use words like Harrison – what do they use as their weapon? There was no doubt that Harrison's intention was to carve into Shelly's heart, on any level he felt he had to. She was indeed selfish, and her response to Oliver's relapse made known to all that she felt his illness was her shame. She cared nothing for Oliver; the only person Shelly cared about was Shelly. In that moment, I felt as though her soul was something I, as a compassionate and caring person could not understand. Breaking into the world of Harrison was enough, but today we were on a long journey into an unknown universe. It was a universe in which laughter became tears; friends went to extremes to help each other; and the true ugliness of the human spirit revealed itself.

Within a couple hours, we packed our bags and loaded the car. We were off to the airport. In my mind, I was wondering when the reservations were made. When we arrived at the small airport, I realized there was no use for reservations. Oliver had his own permanent ride – a Gulfstream jet. Admittedly, I got butterflies. Even though this was a somber event, I was pretty anxious to see what the inside of a private jet looked like; let alone to ride in it.

As we boarded the jet, I can sense anxiety starting to build in Oliver. The Mayo Clinic, to Harrison is like another home. He appreciates it and while he doesn't enjoy having to go there – he is blessed to have a place to go when he needs it. It goes without saying that of all the hospitals in the world, the Mayo Clinic is one of the best places to go.

The flight is quick – too quick in my opinion, and possibly Oliver's. Harrison is perfectly cheery. Oliver, on the other hand is a bit annoyed with Harrison's chipper attitude. Harrison senses this, and slows down the tempo, just a little bit. The plane lands and I feel I have enjoyed the ride. The inside of a private jet is indeed quite nice, but I'm sure I'll remember it better when I'm not in constant motion. Oliver has a black car waiting for us when we land. The car takes us to the Mayo Clinic.

When we arrive on the Psychiatric unit floor, Dr. Ebel meets us. The transition is quick and I am not sure that I understand what is really going on. Dr. Ebel shakes Harrison's hand and Harrison pats Oliver on the back and Dr. Ebel and Oliver walk off.

I look at Harrison and say, "Uh, now what?" Harrison smiles, pats me on the back, as we walk back into the elevator.

"Mason, when a person with a mental illness is in crisis – the only thing we as friends and family can do is provide safety and then get them the professional care that they need. Yesterday was safety, today was getting Oliver the care that he needs."

"Is it that easy?"

Harrison laughed and said: **"NO! There are many more equations in life than just mathematics. When you truly love someone and have compassion, education, and money – it is a lot easier. However, as you will learn throughout this year: for most, those equations are all screwed up and for a lot of my life – they were screwed up. That is when things get sad!"**

As much as Harrison loves the Mayo Clinic, feeling well himself – he is eager to leave and get back home. It is obvious he can't help but look back at all the days he himself has walked through psychiatric unit hallways and had to flail into calisthenics to even get basic needs. Many of those times, Harrison was alone. I guess you could say Harrison didn't have a Harrison. The interesting part of all that is: Harrison set about to see that everyone had a Harrison; at least as many as he could. That is exactly what his whole life became about.

Harrison seems lost in deep thought as we get settled back onto Oliver's jet. After all the years of mental hospitals, institutions and fighting on behalf of the mentally ill; it is still hard for him to believe it was his life. He couldn't help think of the intense difference of dealing with illnesses between the rich and everyone else. There were also similarities. Harrison knew full well what some don't. The smallest of obstacles between you and help can be as devastating as life or death.

It's life or death whether you are rich or poor. If Oliver had to walk to his doctor, or fly on a private jet, the result would have been no different. That is why he called Harrison. He couldn't do it even when he had a private jet – an obstacle is an obstacle. Having someone that loves you more than they hate the illness – is the only ingredient that works.

Harrison did call from the plane to find out what Oliver's Lithium level was. It was at half what it should be. The events had obviously triggered a chemical shift. Harrison reminded himself to check his own lithium level as soon as he gets home.

By the time we get back to Harrison's cabin, Harrison is visibly exhausted. Having had a stressful and trying day, Harrison retires to his bedroom immediately upon coming home.

Chapter 11

Painting

Every day with Harrison is an educational experience on many different levels. He's like a timeless book; the more I experience Harrison, the more I want to discover. He truly is an open book with many such vivid chapters. The more I read, the more I want to know. That's precisely why I feel he has brought me to this place. I feel it's a place for learning; a place for discovery. That's how I felt about this experience. It truly is wonderful.

As I awoke the next morning, Harrison seemed quite excited:

"Today, Mason, I'm going to paint!"

"I wasn't aware you were a painter."

"I'm not, but I love to paint. No one ever understands what the hell it is that I paint! I paint in the drawing room, isn't that clever?" he says laughing.

I can't help but to follow Harrison to the pole barn to see what this painting adventure is going to be about. Sure enough, he has it all. The easels, the paints, the canvasses of every size and a large tool box full of every painting tool you could imagine. I help Harrison carry his supplies to the drawing room.

Harrison then makes a call to the Mayo Clinic to check on Oliver. Everything seems to be going well.

"Hospitals are an amazing place Mason. They introduce you to people that absolutely blow you away with things of the mind."

"You have been hospitalized many times, haven't you?"

"Oh yes, so many for so many different circumstances. We will talk about those as the memories surface. I am going into the drawing room and paint for a while."

As I take a walk, I recall in my research a report that Harrison wrote from a previous hospital stay:

To be here is both comforting and disturbing. Whether my new housemates have illnesses such as: self mutilators, bipolar disorder, schizophrenia, or a mixture of one or the other, I relate to them. There is no explaining or defending to do here. We all know the truth that everything we experience is real whether others hear or see what we do or not – it is real to us.

Shadows cross my heart
I turn to see where they have gone
A voice enters my head
'Your life is all but ruined'
My heart skips a beat
As the pain grows very deep
The shadows are here again
The battle must now begin.

Fighting for ones sanity is quite possibly the hardest thing one has to do as you are the only person who can see or hear the enemy and at times, no one believes it is real. I am considered 'high functioning' here, which you would think is a good thing. However, as any psychologist would tell you, it is a burden to be high functioning. I am aware my mind knows the answers; it is also a constant battle with the demons inside of me.

The 'normals' always want a reason or logic as does my mind, however, logic and reason can be altered in my state of mind to work against me. To be able to defend why you should die better than why you should live is a very distressing position to be in, especially when it appears the benefit is for all... if you die.

I am constantly asked about suicide. It seems that suicide is defined as one act, a gun, pills, cutting or some other act that is isolated. I am not sure I see suicide only in this way. It is possible suicide can be a very long process. Suicide can be a subconscious sabotage on you. You slowly push people you love away, one way or another. You set yourself up for failure until you have given yourself the reason and logic to in fact take your life or die trying.

It was hard to understand the desperation in this essay. It was like two, maybe even more people, inside one. The battle must be excruciating and tortuous, but to the mind! Harrison wrote over one hundred of these reports on many different topics, but most of his essays were about mental illness.

Nearly three hours had passed and Harrison finally emerged on the back deck. His eyes clearly blood shot from tears and his face drawn in stress. He lit up a bit when the boys came to him as if they knew he needed comfort.

"Well young man – I am going to take a walk then we can have some lunch. It will then be time for a nap! You are welcome to look at my paintings if you wish." Harrison strolled off with the boys leading the way as he talked to them affectionately.

I couldn't wait another minute to get into the drawing room to see what he had painted. When I stepped in, the lights had been shut off with the exception of the track lighting with 2 dimly lit spot lights on two canvasses. I was immediately drawn into what I saw.

The canvas on the left had a quarter-sized circle in the center with the brightest gold, yellow and silver colors. It was as brilliant as if a celestial body itself were there on the canvas. The pain seemed to work itself both back and forth to this light with dark clouds of black, gray and silver. The darkness intensified and then lightened sporadically darkening to deep black at the perimeter of the bright center circle. The painting seemed to be alive as if the dark clouds were moving and the light flickered in a three dimensional tunnel.

To the right of the first canvas was a second painting. Although a rectangle, it appeared to be circular with light. There were hues of gold, yellow and silver surrounding the outer canvas and the clouds of billowing black, gray and silver turbulently swirling to the center of a deep black and equally sized circle as the painting on the left.

I simply just stared. Was this what it was like to be in the mind of Harrison? Did this represent now? A time? A place? He said he couldn't paint – but the evidence was of the contrary. Not only could he paint, but with the same veracity of his ability to take words and make then come to life. I stood in the drawing room for nearly an hour. All the paint, brushes, and tools were neatly put away – he was done.

For three hours, Harrison worked intensely on these paintings that exuded moods and emotions – then, the moment was complete.

From behind me, I can hear Harrison ask: **"So what do you think?"**

"I thought you said you couldn't paint?"

"I can't, I can however convert emotions to color as I see them."

"Harrison, these are works of art!"

"Oh, young man, you need to get out more if you think that is art!" He laughs! **"They are named 'The Choice of '08". My mood and my mind battled between the two in a most distressing year. We will take them out to the barn with the others tomorrow."**

"The others?"

"Oh, yes, there are many." Harrison winks and I follow him to the back deck.

Chapter 12

Harrison Discusses Coping Skills

Harrison pours each of us an ice tea.

"Harrison, I must ask you a question about your personality, do you mind?"

"Not at all – shoot!"

"You seem to be able to switch gears easily between sadness and happiness. It is as if you are able to oscillate from one to the other at will! How?"

Harrison drops his head and then raises it and looks at me.

"This is a good observation you have made, Mason. What you have witnessed is not a personality trait, but a coping skill. It has taken me years to develop and it is essential to my survival. When my mind enters a moment or encounters an emotion, I allow myself to feel it and absorb it as intensely as possible. However, the emotions are only allowed the amount of time they need for healthy expression and internal release.

It is then that you see me close the door on the moment and move onto something else. I don't burn the bridge of the moment; that would not be healthy. Yet, to marinate the meat in anything too long destroys the meat. Have no doubt Mason; I have emotions and moments so strong that I could spend the entire year discussing just one. That would be a shame to see only one dimension of a man. Same with life, I don't want people to think I am one dimensional – I am not. I know one dimensional people and they are wonderful people, but quite boring really. That would not be me. Now

it is time for a different moment – it's called a nap!" Quietly, Harrison chuckles to himself. He gets up from his chair and leaves for his bedroom.

It's a coping skill, I think to myself. Harrison has a canny way of simplifying even the most complex things. Yet, he is right. I can't think of any good that has ever come out of 'marinating' in anything too long.

That evening was reflective as I sat and contemplated what it must be like to live the life of Harrison Remy. The next couple weeks were somewhat lighthearted and I simply had the pleasure of getting to know Harrison as a person, today – rather than all he had been through.

I never realized how much I would grow to admire and respect this man the longer I was with him. I learned more as I travelled through what his experiences were.

Chapter 13

Introduction of Lydia

One morning we were seated in the kitchen having coffee and the telephone rang. Harrison answered it:

"Lydia!" Lydia is Harrison's first cousin and closest relative. Many have always said that Lydia is the closest thing to a sibling that Harrison has had throughout his life. Lydia and Harrison are only six months apart.

"Lydia, I just heard from Olivia a few weeks ago. How are you?" He pauses to hear her response. **"Well you're old! How is your husband, Mitch?"** He pauses to wait for her to answer, and then says, laughing: **"Well, he is old as well!"**

"Yes, I will be leaving here in a fortnight. I can't believe another autumn has gone by. Lydia, listen – I want a family reunion next year. Here at the cabin. There are two motels close and plenty of grounds and room here. We will do it the old- fashioned way but with caterers. We are too old for that shit. This is important – no arguments. You are in charge of planning. Now dear, what did you call for?"

"Well of course I am well; I am not as old as you are! Okay we will see you in a couple of weeks. You'll come down for dinner won't you? – all right – cheerio!"

I'm laughing at this conversation somewhat. I wasn't sure if they read each other's minds or they just couldn't hear very well.

"Oh Lydia, she has been a busy body since the day she could see. I figure a family reunion will keep her occupied for the

next 10 months!" Harrison laughs in that ornery laughter, that I've been so fortunate to come to know. He always laughs so fiercely, and with such passion! That was the first odd thing I came to know about Harrison Remy.

"Do you know Mason, Lydia actually locked me in the trunk of a car when we were little? What nerve – I have never forgotten it either!"

"Are you and Lydia close?"

"Oh yes. She and I have two completely different lives, but we are very close. Lydia is solid like a Packard! She doesn't move on her point of view or what she believes in. That has been a very important trait she has, that has helped me throughout my life. I still owe her for the trunk thing though. I would lock her in the Bentley but then I would have to hear about how ridiculous it was to spend that much money on a car for the rest of my life.

Lydia is practical. She could have fifty million in the bank and would not ever change her form. But as you guess, I am bit different and much more eccentric. Especially with money. So Lydia and I don't discuss money!" Harrison laughs again. Sometimes it seems he can't end a sentence without chuckling or laughing.

"Lydia got our grandfathers genes – my dad's dad. They know money and the value of it. To me it has always been a pain the ass. Like I have said before, I spend more money than some people make a year keeping my money separated from me!"

"Do you hate money, Harrison?"

"No – I used to. But my feelings are no longer hatred for money. More so, frustration. I understand the concept of in and out like my grandpa always taught me, but I could never understand the amount I worked and still not having much.

66

Unfortunately, many of my hobbies in life are expensive and so are my tastes! I never quite understood where that expensive taste came from."

"You haven't said much about Ohio yet."

"Well, we will be there in a couple weeks for one thing. The second thing is I have little good to say about my hometown. I don't like it there. If it were not for family, I wouldn't go there. It isn't the state, mind you – not even the county or the land – it just all represents a very bad place in my heart, soul and mind."

I could tell Harrison had no interest in going home, but home was where Lydia and some of the other family still lived and it wasn't the people he felt animosity to, it was the memories.

Chapter 14

The Fire

That evening we were going to make a small bonfire. We thought it would be great to enjoy everyone's company, and celebrate nights that were finally starting to become cool. Harrison declared that the best way to do this was to sit by the fire with smores, franks, and buns. I work with Harrison to get things organized. I like the way he always puts the extra effort in organizing and preparing – because when the enjoyment comes, there is no work to do.

We discussed Oliver's progress, which was going well. Once we had everything organized, we would now take the paint that was left in the drawing room to the pole barn.

When we walk into the pole barn, Harrison rolls back a wall on tracks; and to my astonishment, behind the moveable wall an entire side of the barn is full of paintings! I could feel my heart flutter, as I gazed up a sixteen foot wall. It felt like the conclusion of the most incredible journey my eyes ever experienced. It seemed like a kaleidoscope, radiating out brilliant colors. As I look at these brilliant paintings I see everything from solid black to the most vibrant of reds and sapphire. My eyes instantly started to water as my sense of sight moved me so emotionally. Hell and heaven; peace and torture; hatred and love all encompassed on individual canvasses so vividly expressed on the wall.

Harrison didn't look at me as he said:
"It is a very busy mind, eighty years and I still have not trained it to slow down." I couldn't speak, I felt a tear falling

and I couldn't catch it. My eyes wouldn't blink – they were stunned into absolute ceaseless wonder. "How?" I asked.

"Sometimes you have to go through a very dark place in order to see the light and the color in life!" Harrison said slowly.

Harrison placed the canvases on the wall and turned and walked out without saying another word. I still couldn't move. As I stood there I realized that Harrison's life was like finding a seashell at the beach, buried in sand. I could see maybe the top of it, and as I start to dig it out, I discover that this seashell, that I thought was tiny, is actually much more. Almost as though the grand parts of the shell were still hidden, and I had only experienced the tiniest bit.

On the wall with all the paintings I was moved by the people, places, horrors and honors that came to life in front of me. I stared at this seemingly alive wall of color for a long time, so long that I forgot how long I had been there.

By the time I got back to the house and walked to the back deck, feeling like a zombie, Harrison simply handed me a beer as if to say, "You need this!" I just turned and looked at Harrison who silently looked at me and than river. I had so many questions yet to ask, but I couldn't verbalize one of them. As the sun began to fall, I started to come back to reality. We moved down to the fire pit and Harrison ignited the fire and played with it a bit. As the days light dimmed the fires light built to an amazing roar.

Harrison was staring intently into the fire.

"Hell...people have so many definitions."

The fire seems to dance as it reflects against the glossiness of his eyes.

"Even those who have lived through their own hell have different definitions. I was twenty eight years old. Prison

was a strange place. Some treated it like boy's camp and some like the center of gang relations. Yet some actually treated it with the regard it was meant for – punishment. I had only been there one week. I was trying to feel my way around. I wasn't sure how long I had to stay and for my own sanity, I knew I had to think of a plan of things to do and keep busy. I took a day to walk the building and the grounds. There was a library that was satisfactory, a handball court, gymnasium, ping pong, and a fitness center. One could engage in hobbies if you had the money to order the supplies.

In the center of the prison was a huge courtyard with bleachers on the perimeter, a baseball diamond and a track around the outside. Stairs jetted out of the building every fifty feet or so from the long hallways. I found the infirmary, hoping I never had to go inside there. I found the visiting area and read the instructions.

While walking down the hall, I saw another sign that said, 'outside'. I asked a couple inmates if I was allowed to go through this corridor and I was. I stepped down maybe ten steps then off to the right and through an average door into a small courtyard then another gate that lead to a large fenced in area with no buildings in the way of seeing the outside. This area even had trees. I sucked in the air like I had never experienced oxygen before. It was simply beautiful to me. I thought in my mind how I could use each day. I could walk the track then sit underneath the huge willow tree and write. I could escape into my own imagination here. My mind would be able to transcend this place and I would be able to find some peace.

I spent nearly the entire day out there simply trying to fill my head with good things. On Mondays I could go to the library in the morning and then bring a book out here to read underneath the willow tree. Friday I will walk and write, Saturday and Sunday I would simply relax here in the fresh air. It was hard for me to believe that I was being afforded such a privilege. There is a God, I thought to myself.

There were only a couple other inmates on the yard, my new heaven. I didn't see any officers – just peace and quiet. It was nearing the time that I had to be back for "count".

So you know, Mason, all inmates have to be counted, each day. I knew I had to start making my way back. I passed through the gate into the small courtyard, which seemed to have no purpose. I took another deep breathe. I was so excited that I had found a place like this to find some mental and emotional release. It was a great day.

My right foot stepped into the doorway off the small courtyard that lead up to the stairs to the large main hallway. As I brought my left foot up to fully enter the doorway – something hit my right ear with a strong force and I felt a thump in my ear drum. The hall not was not lit, but did have some natural light spilling in. My head and body were then yanked to the right and my feet scrambled to keep up with my body and find balance. I must have said something in panic as the hand came from my ear to my mouth and I was thrown against the wall."

Staring into the fire so intensely with the flames still reflecting in his eyes, I listened to Harrison with goose bumps throughout my body – he never flinched as he relived that memory verbally. But it isn't just verbal to Harrison, he is seeing it, he is feeling it, in that moment.

"I could only see wall and darkness now with my head pressed against the wall. "Shut the fuck up" a voice said deeply and unforgivingly. I said nothing. I could not see the person, but could feel the strength in his arms and body. I would certainly be no match for him in any physical response.

He stripped my pants from me, pulling so hard that I had bruises down my legs for a week. He manipulated my body like I was a rag doll and I said nothing as he spoke humiliating words that I still hear but don't share. After he was done invading me – he threw me against the wall. I tripped over my pants and fell. I never looked up and he was gone. I am not sure how long I sat there. I pulled my pants up and found it hard to stand up from the pain he had caused. I was bleeding and had incredibly sharp pains throughout my body.

No tears, simply an overwhelming sense of 'I give up'. The emotion of fear was redefined for me in that moment. The world was done with me and all that I loved had turned away from me – at least this is how I felt and now I had just been raped, in prison, with no help. You can't call yourself a victim, when no cares…"

A lump in my throat is actually stifling my breath. I had no idea. No idea at all of the extent of Harrison's experiences and pain. He continued.

"I had to walk slowly, because I couldn't walk any other way and I knew that is was count time. The only thing I needed to worry about was getting to my dorm before count time. I knew the blood had to be visible. I had no way to hide it. I knew I was walking strangely, but tried desperately to walk at a normal pace. Finally making it to my dorm, I felt a sense of relief. Now all I had to do was wait for count to get over and while everyone else went to dinner, I would shower – I never cared to eat again anyway. As I got to the dorm a large woman met me screaming, "And who the hell do you think you are?" It appeared I was very near late and she had blown her whistle early. She went into a long diatribe of how I seemed to think I was better than everyone else. My eyes kept losing focus and I kept seeing the face of so many people that I knew felt the same way as she obviously did.

Her exact words were not registering to me – it was all in the tone. Her final words however, that were said screaming in front of 90 inmates living in the same room as I – were, "Get on your bunk – PUNK!" Keep in mind Mason, "punk" in prison means a person that sells his body for money and safety. I made it to my bunk.

As I laid there, my heart, my soul, my spirit and my mind all separated from my physically being. I couldn't allow any of these elements to come together – they were not allowed to communicate or they would cause an explosion so unpredictable and so very fatal. One of them was going to live the rest would die – I just didn't know which one would survive.

When the dinner bell rang, I made my way to the showers. While the water felt good, I knew nothing was ever going to clean my mind, heart or soul. I wanted my body dismantled and simply thrown away.

In another hour I would have to walk out of the dorm again… it was pill call and I had to have my medication. There I was, of all the times I wanted to be out of it – I was going to go take a medication that was going to make me be in more reality than I had ever been and never let me forget it.

That night, the few times I did shut my eyes, I watched the lawyers and judge and family in my head laughing and celebrating in a courtroom… I relived the assault and never did see the assailant but saw the faces of family and once friends enjoying my pain. This is a visual I have to this day. The next day I actually got a letter from someone telling me just how awful they thought I was."

For nearly two hours straight, Harrison's eyes never moved from the fire. Tears ran down his cheeks, on a face that seemed to age twenty years right in front of me. He told the story in much greater detail – too much to share in this book. As his eyes never moved from the fire; mine never moved from his eyes.

Harrison then stood up. He walked towards the house and getting to me he stopped, looked back at the fire and said:

"I hope there is a hell; I know many who belong there." He took another step, put his hand on my shoulder and said, **"Every night when you go to bed, you thank God that you are safe. Every morning you wake up – you pray to God you will be safe!"** and he continued to the house.

As if the world had stopped, time motionless, the fire roaring and the food laying untouched, I sat there for hours in the most incredible silence, I too hoped there was a hell for all those people.

I cleaned up the pit area and as the fired died down, so did the last of my energy. I lay down in my bed and did, indeed thank God for my safety. I knew my friendship with Harrison had just reached a new level. He had just shared something very intimate with me. It was realism beyond his philosophy – a part of the core that made this man.

I later learned that this abuse went on for six months and as many times as four times per week. The one thing that I took away from Harrison's struggle in prison is that he suffered needless horrors because of that place. As I knew from my archives and research about the man, Harrison's mental illness was the accessory to the crime. He needed help. He needed treatment. Incarceration makes things far worse for people with mental illness, causing needless suffering, anguish and pain. But it is this curse, this bane of society, that we imprison those who are most in need of society's help. We call it "justice".

Chapter 15

The Journey to Ohio

The next couple of weeks went by quickly. I spent a great deal of time writing. Harrison spent his time closing up the house for the year. We will leave for Ohio tomorrow morning.

The morning sun was glistening in the crisp cool air. Leaves were blanketing the ground and the sun was able to shine through the trees. We had a long trip ahead of us. It would be a six hour drive. We loaded up early; Harrison wanted to get an early start. Ruthie was there to see us off and Harrison made one more call to Oliver to see that all was going well.

It was comical to see the boys sitting in the backseat of a Bentley. Dogs are rough on leather. A Bentley is luxurious. But what I keep forgetting is that these dogs were luxurious. They drink beer out of bowls in upscale pubs after exhausting boat rides! On second thought, it didn't seem so out of place for *these* dogs to be riding in a Bentley.

The home in Ohio, which Harrison affectionately called "mom's house" was always well maintained by local people and relatives. Along the way, we will stop at some markets and pick up some groceries and supplies.

After driving for nearly an hour, it was time to get off the highway. I am completely lost, however the GPS and Harrison help me navigate my way through the country roads. We approached a huge wall of hedges that seemed to go on and around forever. They twisted and weaved around the property, and were at least seven feet high, providing wonderful privacy. The hedges stopped at a gate.

Harrison clicked on an opener from the glove compartment and the gate opened. From inside, these huge hedges completely surrounded five acres of yard, barn, pond and orchard. All beautifully landscaped and meticulously maintained.

The home, though not particularly large, was sided in all cedar with beautiful porches. As we walked through the garage, into the house; I was pleasantly surprised to see that Harrison's mother did like pictures! We didn't waste any time getting settled into our respective rooms. Harrison had mentioned on the way that when we got to the Ohio house, the first thing we do is get comfortable, settled and take a nap before dinner.

Harrison did just that. I on the other hand took liberty with my freedom and walked around the house taking in the pictures of so many people that I had been hearing about for the past couple of months. People that were more a part of Harrison and his history than anyone could be.

There were pictures of family and extended family. Harrison's family, while being a traditional mid-western family, was also a good looking family. All the framed pictures were marked on the back with little labels. I found several pictures of Lydia who indeed looked like she could be Harrison's sister. I saw pictures of Harrison's parents throughout the years who were photographed in places all over world, participating in adventurous activities. They were obviously very active in their lives.

When I walked into what was a more formal living room in the house, is when I came across many young photos of Harrison. All seemed to be typical family photos of an only child. I saw pictures of a boy who was blond-haired and blue-eyed. It was impossible for me to not look into Harrison's eyes in each photo and not reflect back to his stories. One particular gave me chills.

There was a profile photo of Harrison. In this photo, Harrison represented everything one would think of him in his twenties.

He was in Monte Carlo overlooking the bay of Monaco. No smile, just a serious stare out to the horizon. Harrison was a traditionally good looking man with strong European features. When I turned the photo frame over to see the age, I nearly dropped the frame. The photo was of Harrison at the age of 25, only three years prior to the story he had told me by the fire in Michigan.

As I looked into the photo of someone that appeared to have it all – it was impossible to not flashback to the vivid details of Harrison's first assault in prison. What must this be like for someone who actually lived it?

I continued walking through the home and looked out over the farm land to the large hedged trees that surrounded the entire property.

Chapter 16

Family Gathering

It was only a few hours and many things are running through my mind as Harrison appeared in the kitchen.

"My grandfather always called this house a museum."

"I can see why!"

"Well, it won't be more than an hour before some people start showing up, I assure you. If you need to freshen up or anything now is a good time."

"Who's coming over?"

"It's always hard to tell!"

Within the hour, the gates opened up and several people came through the front door, the garage door and the basement doors. Everyone seemed to know this house just as well as Harrison did. As Harrison spent time introducing people to me, I gradually learned that these were all first and second cousins that Harrison had grown up with. There was definitely a familial closeness, yet I also sensed a detachment.

During the conversations I noticed that the collective memories of Harrison stopped when Harrison was eighteen; and his relationships with his relatives changed.

It was obvious that Harrison navigated towards Lydia and stayed close to her regardless of the conversation. I wouldn't say that Harrison was uncomfortable around his family; however he was very observant rather than participatory. It was with Lydia that he spoke with unguarded openness. Everyone was either in their eighties or close to it. It was interesting that so many cousins were all born at the same time; I couldn't help but think there had been something in the water around here back then.

The gathering lasted only a few hours and people gave their hugs and said their farewells. It was clear that this was a once a year event and Harrison would not be seeing any of them until the following year. I found it somewhat sad that a year could be summed up in a three hour get together with family, but I also had a keen sense that this was Harrison's preference. When Lydia finally left, Harrison and I retired to the basement sitting room.

"Harrison, why the hedges around the property?"

"Well, as I said, I'm not comfortable in this area of the world. I'm very comfortable in this home and on this property – so one of the first things I did when I had money was dividing the two."

It was obvious the hurt Harrison related to this area. It was also obvious how much he loved this home and everything inside of these shrub walls. This was home to him, no matter where it was located.

"Is it hard to come back here?"

"Oh no. There are wonderful memories here at this house and surrounding homes and places. I have not set foot in town for nearly thirty-five years, however and I have no intention of doing so."

Harrison's comment about never setting foot into town here in Ohio was in stark contrast to the time I spent with him in

Michigan. In Michigan going into town was a ritual. He knew everybody, and everybody wanted to be around him. He said hello to the townspeople, the shopkeepers, and even the bartenders.

In Ohio, he preferred to remain anonymous. It was almost as though this space was the only place he trusted. Inside the hedges, he was comfortable. Beyond the hedges was the unfamiliar. I wondered if it was because he didn't want to be confronted by someone who knew the secret I felt he was hiding. Was it that? Or was it something deeper?

We retire for the evening and I once again, I lie down in bed, confused by the paradox that is Harrison Remy. But as I've learned as I've studied some of the most powerful advocates in American history; greatness does not come without complexity. And Harrison was indeed complex.

Chapter 17

Lydia and Harrison through the Years

Throughout the next morning the telephone rang many times. People were calling to check in and touch base. There are many gadgets here. I see some of the most modern electronics, including flatscreen televisions that stretch the width of the walls. They rotate through different paintings and other forms of art. Some are themed with the house, but every so often I catch a Matisse or Van Gogh; a Picasso or a Gauguin. Music is playing some of the best works of; Bach, Beethoven and Chopin. The house is filled with the aroma of chili made from scratch, and the smell of coffee is wonderful. I can even smell a hint of cinnamon to compliment the aroma of the brewing coffee. Everything matches in this house. It's so well done I mention it to Harrison.

"Yes, it was designed by the firm, Mom and Dad, Inc," he says, chuckling at his answer.

He explained how everything about the house, right down to the cabinets and bathroom sinks were built and designed by his parents.

The bell rings and the television in the kitchen switch to a view of the outside gate.

"Ah – Lydia!" He pushes a button on the wall, and from the television I see the gate opening. Shortly, in walks Lydia through the garage. She was so calm and radiated all the pleasant things

Harrison ever said about her. In short she was consistent and stable.

Harrison and Lydia sat and talked about people I'd never heard of, yet I find it all very interesting. Harrison has great concern for those experiencing any tribulations in the family. He also has laughter and happiness for those enjoying their time in life. They recall their grandparents and the older generation of their youth. They grew up quite close and knew each other well.

Lydia talks of her children, grandchildren and now great grandchildren. The way they talk, it seems for the both of them that they can't believe they're so old to even be discussing great grandchildren. Lydia asks me if I can find anything at all interesting enough to write about Harrison. At first, her dry humor convinced me that she was serious. I replied by saying, "I could write a book right now!" Lydia says, "I have no doubt about that, just remember he is bullheaded!"

"ME!" Harrison exclaims, giggling and rolling his eyes, and then offers a playful retort: **"Bullheaded?"**

"I have been trying to get this woman to South Africa for over thirty years and she won't go. I can't even get her to Paris, and I'm the one who's bullheaded?"

Lydia cackles at Harrison's response and points a finger in his direction, and offers her philosophy on world travel.

"There is no reason to go to Paris, Harrison. South Africa sounds great, but it is entirely too far and Mitch does not like to fly."

It is obvious they have been having this same conversation for decades.

"At least Olivia came to South Africa. The only family I could get there. She brought the kids about ten years ago.

We did the whole South African experience. Safari, Sun City, Johannesburg, Pretoria, Durban, the Blue Train to Cape Town, all of it. We spared no expense!"

Lydia pipes in. "Yes, NO expense was spared. The kids thought people just live that way – in first class all the time!"

"Well, Lydia, some do, you know!" Harrison says laughing and the bickering continues.

"Gramps would have a complete fit at how much money you spent on that train ride alone!" Lydia exclaims.

"Lydia, it is the second most luxurious 'train ride' in the world next only to the Orient Express."

"Amtrak, Blue Train, Orient express – what the hell is the difference besides champagne and thousands of dollars? It is like that damn car you have!" As Lydia gets up to pour a cup of coffee and sneaks a wink to me!

Harrison looks at me with overt orneriness. **"By the way Lydia, I wanted to show you something about my car."**

I couldn't believe my ears and had to excuse myself to the restroom. I was fighting back laughter. Surely he wouldn't! She's 80 years old!

When I came back into the room, the two of them were gone. I ran out to the garage and there stood Harrison grinning wickedly, like a cat who destroyed an antique piece of furniture. He was leaning against the trunk of the Bentley!

"Harrison, where is she?" I exclaimed.

"Her geriatric ass is busy figuring out the interest I could have made on the money that I spent on this car – but from

inside the trunk! Damn this feels good. Seventy years, I waited seventy years to do this!"

I immediately open the driver's door and press the trunk release and need to nearly pick her up to get her out of the trunk. As Lydia steps out, dignified and composed she says, "You would think a car that cost as much as a house would have a release button from inside the trunk or at least lights!" Everyone bursts into laughter.

As we head back inside, Harrison says: **"You know damn well you are a closeted first class girl, Lydia!"**

I say, "Have you ever traveled first class Lydia?" I'm still laughing about the fact Harrison locked her in the trunk and then her response was as Harrison predicted.

"Yes, Harrison took me on the Boeing 777 in first class and it was simply ridiculous!"

"OH MY GOD – YOU LOVED IT and YOU KNOW IT!" and the bickering was on again. They loved to do little things that aggravated one another. It was visible however, in this bickering, the true respect they had for one another and for their lives. Harrison could no more have lived Lydia's life than Lydia could have lived his – but they appreciated that in one another.

It was nearly one o'clock in the afternoon as Lydia said: "Let's have a glass of wine – you've gotten me stressed out!" Harrison jumps up and grabs a bottle of wine, looking on the bottom, the top and all the way around for a price – not wanting Lydia to see that it is most likely a good wine. Harrison pours us each a glass.

"You two are wonderful to watch!" I say in excitement.

It wasn't long before the old photo albums were covering the breakfast bar in the kitchen. Harrison had a lightness about him that I had not seen. It was obvious he did not carry any pretentions about himself around Lydia. All afternoon we looked at photos and they told their stories. Harrison said, "**She was so bossy!**" Lydia responded with, "He was so careless!"

Lydia asked if Harrison would join in on Thanksgiving this year.

"Lydia, you know I don't do Thanksgiving around anyone. I go to the cemetery and sulk in self-pity."

Lydia bows her head and says, "It doesn't have to be that way."

"It is that way!"

The conversation of the past and life in general goes well into the evening. The next day we would all be traveling to Olivia's house for brunch.

Chapter 18

Olivia's House

9:30 AM came early, after a great day of absorbing all I could from the conversation between Harrison and Lydia. Mitch and Lydia were ready and I drove Harrison's car through the gates and less than a mile to Mitch and Lydia's home. From Mitch and Lydia's house, the drive takes nearly an hour to Olivia's.

As we drive into the development, it is obvious that Olivia and her husband Blair are doing well for themselves. They are both doctors. The home is large, on the golf course, yet not pretentious. Harrison's eyes light up when he sees Olivia standing at the portico waiting.

"Hello Hello Hello!" Harrison exclaims as he steps out of the car. We follow into the home which is simply beautiful. Understated class is how I would describe it. Olivia asks us all into the dining room. The table is set elegantly. Everything is perfect. You can see Olivia giving glances to Harrison to make sure he is impressed. Harrison is not only impressed but basking in pride of his goddaughter.

Brunch was incredible and we all enjoyed light conversation. Harrison asked about Eleanor, Lydia's eldest daughter. She was doing well and very busy. Harrison looks at me.

"Eleanor is a scientist in Columbus. I love her, but when she talks work, I have not a clue what she is saying, it is all Swahili to me!"

Lydia smiles, as she interrupts Harrison:

"Greek! Harrison, it's all Greek to you. Not Swahili."

"It may be Greek to you, but I speak Greek, so that wouldn't make much sense, now would it?"

Lydia rolls her eyes, yet grins at the same time shaking her head.

Suddenly Harrison jumps up from his seat, and gestures to the group:

"Can we get out of this formal, fancy dining room and go into the kitchen? A kitchen is where a family should gather."

Everyone must have been thinking the same thing. Each person stood up, and grabbed his or her plates and utensils from the table and we were off to the kitchen.

"Much better!" Harrisons says, as he looks at Mitch and Lydia: **"Are you two golfing today?"**

"Not today, we thought we would be entertained by you and Lydia instead!" Mitch says. The time passes idly by, as we enjoy such good company. We laugh, share stories and tell a few good jokes. We spend time in the kitchen catching up. Olivia then suggested that we head over to the country club deck for cocktails.

Sitting on the deck, Olivia smiles and says, "Remember the Golf course race?" Everyone sits up and starts laughing.

"What was the golf cart race?" I say. Olivia begins the story:

"Oh my..." Olivia starts. "Mom and Harrison were discussing driving and age. The conversation soon got a little competitive. Harrison, looking down from the deck said, "Prove it!" – "Prove what?" mom said. "Prove you can drive better than me!" Harrison said, pointing at the golf carts. "FINE! I will!" Mom said stomping towards the carts. Remember, mom was old and so was Harrison. He was 75 years old! Mom was charging towards the carts and Harrison right behind her. They get into two different golf carts, paying NO attention to the fact that neither cart belonged to us! Mom pulls out – Harrison pulls up beside her. They stare at one another with determination. Meanwhile four different people come off the deck saying, "What are you doing those are our golf carts!" Simultaneously, Harrison and Mom say, "Oh shut up!" Harrison floors it – Mom does the same! Golf clubs go flying, with balls dropping from every side of the carts. Everyone on the deck of the country club is standing at this point and they disappeared across the course. Shortly after, we see them coming. Mom is in the lead by a foot as they return to their starting point. Not a word was said as they stopped. Mom won and the two of them stomped back up to the deck. Harrison ordered a Martini, Mom a wine cooler. Neither one said a word about it, as if it didn't just happen! Harrison starts a conversation that has nothing to do with anything we just saw, and the day went on while the rest of us were about to bust out in laughter."

Harrison says, **"It was the potato salad!"**

Lydia says, "What?"

"That afternoon you made lunch and you made potato salad. It tasted just like Grams."

"I made it for you, you old fart!" Lydia says.

"I know – I have tried to make it that way for fifty years and couldn't – you did, it pissed me off and that is why I was competitive that day!" Harrison says very matter a fact.

"You're a freak!" Lydia says laughing

"You're riding home in the trunk!" Harrison says, also laughing and we all just sit there in hysterics at these two who jab and punch all in the name of love.

Once again, it was an absolutely wonderful day with Harrison and his family. Everyone is tired on the way back to the house and when we get home, Harrison and I meet in the downstairs living room.

Chapter 19

Harrison talks about Family Relations

As we sit, and have a nice cup of decaf I ask Harrison, "It surprises me that you don't spend more time here with your cousins. You seem very close."

"Every year, I have all this to look forward to. Plus, it is during the holidays. The family is big and everyone is extremely busy. My mother had siblings, my dad had a siblings and each of their families all grew. My parents had nieces and nephews and so on. I don't have that – I am just a cousin to everyone and always will be."

"What are your feelings about family, Harrison?"

"That question is very hard to define. Family is not guaranteed nor is family limited to people who share your DNA. I learned that the hard way. Growing up, I believed that family was a guarantee and that family would always be by your side. Friends would come and go, but family would always be there. That is not the case for most and it was not the case for me.

I think that through it all, a ten year span, where I spoke to hardly anyone in this family and they didn't speak to me, we all learned something about life and family.

Mental illness has a unique way of tearing a family apart. Had I been diagnosed with cancer and it cost hundreds of

thousands of dollars to keep me alive, I would have the relationship with my family that one would think I would have. With mental illness, that isn't the reality. Did I ever tell you how I ended up in that prison, Mason?"

"Not from your point of view."

"Well, without getting into all details, I will simplify it. At the age of 28 I owned a travel agency and I bankrupted it from irresponsible and sporadic, eccentric spending. Many people lost their money for a while. It cost my parents a great deal of money and it cost, well – our relationship. It was discovered and diagnosed that it was all caused by symptoms of a mental illness called bipolar disorder. An illness that most in my family did not take seriously and nearly all in the community looked at as an excuse for bad behavior. I was prosecuted for fraud or theft.

The prosecutor and judge were quite adamant about destroying me and when I look back at who actually showed up in that court room that day of sentencing, I knew most of the people I ever loved, felt the same way. Thus began a journey into a world I had no concept of and a complete shift in all that I thought was real."

"This is what caused the ten year separation from your parents and family?"

"Yes, but it was much more than all that. It changed me forever. It changed everything that I was or thought I was. It did not change me in a good way, it nearly destroyed me, killed me and in some sense – it did kill huge parts of me."

"Mental illness is often viewed as an excuse for bad behavior, isn't it?"

"More times than not, Mason, it is. What people do not understand is the fact that this perception kills and it does nothing to help anyone. Frankly, I often view it as an excuse to not get involved. The prison system isn't affecting those that set out to do crime or that have behavioral issues. Those people can easily withstand the judgments inflicted on them by society and family. It kills people that have a conscience, and have a mental illness and I assure you, more times than not, it is seems much easier to die then to face hatred and see the backs of all those you cherished or wanted to be a part of their lives as they walk away."

"Is this how you still feel?"

"My emotions about the situation sway from objectivity and understanding; to hurt and fear. You can't dowse hurt and fear with anger. You must dowse it with love. That is much easier said than done, especially when it is not returned in any way. Just as a person must get sick of being sick in order to enter a recovery for mental illness, a person must get tired of being angry, in order to let it go and not be angry any more. It was Hemmingway that wrote, 'Sooner or later I knew I had to get over it all or it would destroy me.'

"The fact of the matter, Mason is that I did understand the logistics of my family and friends response to my behavior. What I had to learn throughout the years was that my behavior was not logical for a reason. I learned that only by educating myself about my mental illness. I went on a roller coaster of self-discovery and education about my illness and how it worked itself in my life. That took years and a whole lot more mistakes. Very few in my family or circle of friends went through a journey of understanding or education, they simply turned their backs."

"However, like I said, I do have some understanding as to why. Fear, anger, resentment and most importantly I had hurt two people [my parents] more than anyone could have ever hurt them. My family did not take kindly to that and never did."

At first, I felt that I would come home and prove them all wrong. I would become a success, an advocate and make change for people whose lives reflected mine and theirs. It didn't take long to realize that that boat had sailed and no one was interested in what I could do or would do."

"I, myself have never been good at forgiveness. My attitude and actions towards forgiveness do not always match my belief system. I believe you must forgive. I struggle with that at times because letting go of that seems to somehow say that they are right and if they are right, who am I? If I forgive and they are then right – am I only worthy of hospitals, prisons and homelessness? To combat that issue – I constantly talk myself through an affirmation of forgiveness with the hopes that those chains can be released. More times than not, they are. Forgiveness, Mason, is not something you do for someone else. Forgiveness is what you do for your own soul."

"For years, I must admit, I wanted revenge on people that hurt me. The rapists, the family, the friends, the system in general – but I was reminded of a Chinese proverb: 'If you are going to seek revenge, dig a grave for two!' So much of me had died in the process of getting well. I had lost everything that I knew and I lost so much of myself. I was tired of being in pain and I was the only person that could change that dynamic in my life. One must take responsibility for their life – you cannot control or take responsibility for another's life."

"When you came back here, Harrison –your family did welcome you didn't they?"

Harrison chuckles, **"Hmm, I guess that depends on how you define 'welcome'. My family did not welcome me home. They welcomed the fact that my parents had their son home and that my parents were finding peace and happiness again. I was the piece in the puzzle; there was no emotional tie to my presence. When nearly everyone looks at you simply as the prodigal son and has no concept of mental illness and the battle that ensues – they can't possibly detach me from the illness. I assure you there was no sympathy for me."**

"But you are close to Lydia and your cousins…"

"Lydia yes! I trust her completely. Close is not how I would describe the relationship with others. I love them and I believe that they love me or parts of me or maybe the fact they are supposed to love me. But we are strangers. We had all changed considerably by the time I came home. I changed the most because I my entire core was changed. Their lives changed for many reasons as well but they all had families by then and responsibilities to those families. I understood that. I was sad and I was hurt that I didn't feel a part of that, but I realized I simply wasn't a part of it and was never going to be."

"You must realize that even had I never gone through the challenges with my illness, I was a man in my late thirties who had experienced the world. I wasn't just a guy that went on a lot of vacations; I had truly experienced the world and lifestyles that would most likely never cross the paths of most in my family. My life, in general, was hard to relate to. Then you add all that happened; mental illness, prison, homelessness, assaults and everything that goes with it and

you wind up with a "where does one begin" situation. No one was really interested in beginning and looking back. No one ever asked what I had gone through."

"You overcame some incredible obstacles right after coming home! You were an advisor to the Ohio Supreme Court, a writer, a successful speaker, and really reached out to the mental health community with your experiences in a positive light – how could people not notice this?"

"What people notice is an equation. I had always gotten to a level of success no matter how far I had been knocked down. I always got back up again and fought like a son-of-a-bitch to regain my stand in the world. I had a hell of an ego, let me tell you!" Harrison said, shaking his head in disgust.

"People didn't trust my success because they didn't trust me. They didn't trust that I would sustain. A person doesn't invest in what they don't trust. I can't say I blame them really. However, what people don't look at, often times, is the totality of a circumstance. They don't take an aerial view. People tend to stand guard in a protective manner waiting for the other shoe to drop. They go to church, say their prayers and never extend a hand. They come home, they judge and they label and always stand a safe distance away".

"Every flashback that I had in the recent years of my return home, flashbacks of the assaults, were the faces of people that turned their backs – not the faces of the rapists themselves. That was not a conscious decision of mine. So nearly every week or so I would have these flashbacks and by the time I crawled out of bed in the morning I was so emotionally hurt and damaged that I couldn't even see straight. I do not like the emotion of hate – it is poison to the core. However, without a choice, I woke up with such hatred and pain. I could not fathom how so many people that watched me grow up and knew me – could hate me so much. I could not understand how this illness was able to redefine me and leave me for dead in the hearts of so many."

"Years upon years of therapy, medication and prayer have helped me redefine what my choice in all this really is. My regimen of medication, therapy and case management is the army against this illness. If anyone thinks that they are stronger than the illness by themselves, they are truly fooling themselves. I set about changing the paradigm in my life and I knew that I had to have help. I was fortunate; I had my parents to help facilitate that need after 10 years of trying to do it on my own."

"Harrison, I feel that I must tell you something." Harrison looks at me intensely and I become nervous. "Harrison, my uncle has bipolar disorder. He is now 45 years old and his troublemaking weighed heavily on our family, with his behavior and his inability to maintain a discipline in recovery. I have watched for years while he has taken his brother and my father for money and hurt them tremendously. I have hated my uncle for years because of this. Yet, I admire you and respect you for your discipline."

Harrison continues to stare at me and says slowly… **"I find it a shame that you feel you know me better than you know your uncle."**

I am a little taken aback by this response. "I do know my uncle!" I said with confidence.

"No, you know his behavior, Mason – I highly doubt you know your uncle at all. I have met far too many people with mental illness to not know that there is something that the illness feeds off of. Yes, mental illness is chemical; however it generally feeds off of something. Whether it's insecurity,

emotional pain, or something else, it always preys upon the weak and the callow. It would do you well to get to know your uncle.

It doesn't hurt to keep your distance. I am not saying financially support him, a hug doesn't cost anything nor does an, "I love you!" If you and your family isolate your uncle in a silo of shame and guilt – there is nothing but sadness in his future. And Mason, never be shy about opening up to me – nothing shocks me or surprises me in this world."

I actually had a sense of relief after opening up to Harrison. The journey with my uncle will by my own journey and it is my hope that Harrison will continue to teach me more about his journey and that in turn might help me understand more about my uncle. It has been a long day and we retire for the evening.

Chapter 20

Thanksgiving Day

Thanksgiving morning was sunny and bright. It was a beautiful morning; a fitting way to begin the holiday. Harrison was enjoying his coffee, and making a call to the Mayo Clinic to speak with Oliver. He's done so twice a week, ever since Oliver admitted himself after his relapse. The doctors feel as though Oliver is doing very well. Oliver himself said he was doing well and mentioned his immediate future plans. Oliver was to be discharged on December 1st. He felt the holidays were to be too depressing in the States and is planning to be in Paris, or Neuilly, where is home is, outside Paris. I listened while Harrison asked if being alone was a good idea, even in Paris. He added that Oliver was welcome to come to Ohio. Oliver insisted Paris was where he needed to be. He said he might even start writing again. Harrison let him know to call at least twice per week and that he would see him in Paris in January.

As Harrison put down the receiver of the telephone, I couldn't help to notice, even with his cheerful voice that he was not convinced Oliver's plans were a good choice. I asked Harrison how he felt Oliver was doing and Harrison said, **"Not as well as his genius has convinced his doctors he is doing!"** and just shook his head.

Harrison went to his room to get ready for the day. When he returned he was dressed in his finest casual outfit. He had on a black jacket and a thick gray turtleneck with dark jeans. I was surprised that a man who was so old could be so stylish. We were going to spend Thanksgiving Day driving around to some of the cemeteries and visit the graves of his relatives. I thought it an odd thing to do on Thanksgiving; however Harrison would explain that on our drive.

"Gratitude, Mason, is one of the single most important things you can have in your life. This is exactly why I travel to the burial sites of those that have had such a direct impact on my life, my gratitude for them and their lessons."

As we drive into town, we stopped in a cemetery across from the elementary school, to pay tribute at a very important tombstone. I see the name "Remy" at the top of the monument.

"This is my great grandmother Remy and her husband. I never knew him but I always admired him because he came to this country when his entire family in Belgium probably felt he was out of his mind for leaving Belgium. My great grandmother, however, I knew quite well. I would generally spend every day that school was cancelled with her. I even recorded her stories. She was like a radio version of the history channel. I would sit in awe as she told stories about the war in Belgium and how her family survived. It was remarkable to me the perseverance and determination that she had at such a young age. She taught me a lot, but that perseverance is what I kept close to my heart."

We then continued to another cemetery, this one out in the country. Once again, I saw the name "Remy".

"These are my dad's parents. It is hard to define the impact they had on my life. I generally felt as though I always let them down because I was so abnormal and they were so genuine and so real. We always got along and I spent a great

deal of my youth with them, but I was different and they knew it - yet they never actually made me feel that way. My grandfather would try to teach me how to farm and I did not like farming, though I did it. I don't think he could understand how one could not like farming, but it just wasn't my thing for one reason or another. I lost my grandfather while I sat in jail. I am not going to recount those emotions today."

We continued on, even deeper into the country, down a long winding road and up to a cemetery on the river bank. It was a beautiful setting. Harrison and I exited the car and Harrison walked up to the riverbank and looked out on the water. It seemed he was saying a small prayer or meditating. After he had his moment of peace, he walked to a small white tombstone.

"A vault of dust. That is what we all eventually become," Harrison said, bluntly, with a great heaviness to his voice. He then lay down beside the tombstone and said, **"This is where I will be one of these days!"** and grins at me. I didn't know whether to laugh or cringe.

He then just sat by the stone and seemed to be organizing the small landscaping around it a bit. The moment seemed to be over and he moved on to his mother's parents' stone. You could see sadness as he stared intensely at his grandmother's name. **"She would have loved my life."** He then moved to a beautiful stone or monument if you will. It was his parents.

Harrison's parents and he enjoyed life thoroughly over the last couple of decades. They were able to see his success and were instrumental in helping Harrison and thousands of parents come to an understanding of mental illness.

They lived, they enjoyed. They appreciated every moment of their lives together.

"No one helped us figure out how to cope and survive with mental illness. We screwed up many times. Years, actually, and it was painful as hell. So when we finally "got it" by the help of the National Alliance on Mental Illness' Family-to-Family program, we became one. And, every moment since that point, we appreciated every sunrise and every sunset. We fought feverishly for others and forced ourselves even when we were exhausted to live in the moment and thank God we had it."

"The last twenty years of my parent's life we had everything we wanted or needed. We lived. Sure if we wanted to stay in the Ritz in Paris, we would, but those things didn't cross our minds unless there was an occasion to do so. We were very happy in Michigan, at the cabin. We loved horseback riding in Wyoming and Colorado. We all loved the rodeo circuit and followed it. We appreciated our lives to the core. I think the Rodeo Championships in New York City were always a testament to our respect and appreciation of one another's differences. We always stayed at the Plaza. This reflected all of our appreciation for comfort. The morning would consist of mom and I having a light breakfast at the hotel while dad opted for a coffee mug and a stroll through Central Park."

"We would meet after breakfast and start a walk down to the Gardens where the rodeo took place. Dad would spend an hour or so choosing and fitting a new Stetson hat, a tradition that would find my dad's closet full of hats that he would wear once a year, the day he bought it! Mom and I would give our opinions regarding color and style while my mind was thinking of finding boots for him. That would be our next venture, every time. He was now in his official Marlboro man gear. "

"When we got the Gardens, a luxury we afforded ourselves was VIP seating. By 2 o'clock in the afternoon we were enjoying the competition. Generally, we would sit and have a cold beer while the crowds would clear to exit the building.

To keep the mood alive, we would take a cab to a western bar and enjoy some good music along with the occasional mechanical bull ride. Mom preferred quiet dinners so we would find a nice restaurant and enjoy great food and time together.

The following day, mom and dad would do New York their way and I'd do New York my way. My way was to spend the entire day at the MET. Their way was discovering things about New York that I'm not sure even New Yorkers knew. By four o' clock we would meet for a light dinner and I was always amazed at what new adventure they found in the concrete jungle."

Harrison wavered between tears and laughter when he reminisced about his parents.

"We were all three very different people, but we celebrated that difference in one another!"

Harrison then went silent and moved to the riverbank. He was so close to the water; if he took another step he would certainly fall in.

"It is hard for me to believe that I am the last one standing."
Turning back towards the car, he pops the trunk. In the trunk he has a folding table, chairs, table cloth, food service and a bunch of snacks. As we sat and snacked in the cool, but sunny air, Harrison told stories of Michigan Rummy, Christmases, and summers at his grandparent's farm. It always amazed me how Harrison lived in the moment.

I was beginning to wonder about Harrison's coping skills for mental illness were not a philosophy all should adapt in life, not just the mentally ill. When Harrison mourned, he mourned. When he laughed, he laughed from the depths of his being. I believe this is one thing that made him successful, his ability that he calls, 'the movie in my mind' that he adapted to himself from the musical, 'Miss Saigon'.

What seemed to be a sad day was actually a beautiful day. I was comfortable around Harrison at this point and celebrated his free heart and spirit. We packed up and were on our way back to the house.

Chapter 21

Questions and Answers

That evening Harrison afforded me a "free for all in questions" as he called it. So we sat in the downstairs living area. Harrison laughed as he said, "You provide the Q's and I will provide the A's!"

"I realize that you were in prison, but many have been in prison. Where did your passion come from and why? It would have been very easy for you to simply walk away, publish your books, poetry and essays and move on. Instead, you chose to become an advocate and challenge an entire system."

"Yes, I did make a conscious choice to take on the system. I reflect back on a quote I once heard, 'The pain is real but the sense of purpose is much larger.' In essence, I didn't think I had a choice, really. My experiences in prison were horrific. I was consumed by disbelief and fear. I couldn't get my arms around it. What I did find, was a common thread. Respect! A majority of the inmates didn't even know what it was, yet they demanded it in all the wrong ways.

My experiences in prison were much more than that first assault. I was assaulted by as many as eight men at a time four to five times per week. Much more violently than the first assault. I knew I could not change. However, there were things that I did not accept.

The treatment that I received in prison was below par. The first day I went to get my medication, none of the pills were identifiable to me. I wasn't going to take pills that I didn't know what they were! When I acknowledged to the nurse that these did not look familiar she said: 'Are you stupid?' then the officer who stands guard of the medication line, says: 'Take them or go to the hole.'

The timeline for medications, doctor's appointment and so on, were ridiculous to say the least. Nothing followed suit and no one followed through on anything. Any doctor, psychologist or therapists who treated a patient in this manner outside those gates would lose their license for life. Yet, in prison there is no accountability. That made no sense to me. The treatment of the staff of the prison was much more discouraging to me at the time, than the rapes even were because I expected more of the staff and they behaved just as bad, if not worse than the inmates themselves.

The behavior of many corrections officers was deplorable. Nurses and even staff of the mental health department were stigmatizing and generalizing mental illness. I was called everything from crazy, nuts and many more things I don't want to repeat. In the meantime, my life was being threatened if I spoke of the rapes. No one ever spent enough time with me to maybe realize that something was going on.

At one point I was under suicide watch. If that wasn't enough to make you suicidal, I am not sure what is. The conditions were ridiculous. While I understood some of the measure that needed to be taken in order to prevent one from taking their own life, the one thing I could not comprehend was the fact that immediate medical attention was not given. The other factor was the fact that they had corrections officers that had absolutely no understanding of mental illness stationed in that position. I was taunted by corrections officers. That doesn't even make any sense!

I could not understand how, in the year 2000's, this is how we handled mental illness in the criminal justice system. First and foremost, I could not understand why people with non-violent crimes, with mental illness were even incarcerated in a prison.

The fact is Mason, is how ignorant do you have to be to not realize that incarcerating non-violent mentally ill people in a violent prison is damaging. One only needs to look at statistics. I guess if you are truly daft, you could look at the financial cost that this has on any state and our society. Of course, you can't identify the true insanity, which is that I, a non-violent felon, was sent to prison to be raped! Not to mention that a big contributor to my felony was a mental illness."

Chapter 22

Defining Mental Illness

"Harrison, what does mental illness mean to you?"

"That is a loaded question, Mason. Bipolar is the only thing I fear in life. It has been a much larger war to fight mental illness than the elements around it. I think it is impossible to truly comprehend, unless you live it. Although, you would need to be blind, deaf and dumb to not realize the effect it has on the person suffering with it. The sad thing is that society and the stigma around mental illness have been just as devastating to the person living with mental illness as mental illness itself."

"This has had an impact on you as well?"

"Oh my, yes. People have devastated me at times. You have asked why I felt I had to speak up and out about the treatment of the mentally ill – well, I knew one thing and that one thing was, if I lived through all of that, I would have a voice and I would be damn sure to use it.!"

I asked Harrison why he had never gone on to pursue higher education in the field of psychology.

"I did consider that path, Mason. Then I realized that first and foremost, I didn't know if I could conform enough to do so. That was a personal observation.

The professional observation was that I didn't want to lose sight of what was truly important to me. What was

important to me was that all these people that I had met, had a voice.

There are many who have a mental illness and are mental health professionals and I applaud them – I just did not feel that that was my calling."

Chapter 23

Change of Plans

It was the 29th of December. It was a day I'll never forget. We had a small gathering at the house on the 26th for Christmas and everything went well. Harrison and I were scheduled to fly out for New York City. It was Lydia's birthday, therefore Harrison wanted to stop and have brunch with Lydia and Mitch.

We were enjoying brunch and it was obvious the two were going to miss one another. Lydia did agree to come to New York City before we left for Europe. This was something she would often do. About two hours into brunch, as we chatted over coffee and cheesecake, Lydia's telephone rang. It was Ruthie for Harrison.

All I heard was the following: **"Ruthie, what on earth are you calling here for? – Oh God, my God, I didn't think it would happen this soon. I am fine, I will be fine. There is much to do. I must go now – Goodbye."**

When Harrison turned around he had a look that I never saw before. He was more focused than a pair of binoculars. His eyes were vibrant, bright and ice blue. His left eyebrow raised and a stare that was as if directly at someone through all of us. It was actually frightening.

"Harrison, what is it?" Lydia said with great concern.

Harrison turned to look at Lydia without even blinking: **"Oliver's dead. He's in Paris – it was all too much – I hoped he would wait until I got there so that I could help him fight. FIGHT! Like all of us with mental illness have to do. Mental**

illness is a war; it's a battle! It's something you cannot let control you. You must control it. Excuse me friends, I must go."

Lydia's eyes immediately filled with tears. Oliver's life had resembled Harrison's life in so many ways throughout the years. Their success in the battle against mental illness had fed one another. Lydia's eyes were also filled with fear. She had fought hard for Harrison for many years. While Lydia and Harrison always bicker, it was also very clear that Lydia had always put up with all the bullshit that went along with Harrison's illness. She wasn't just someone that stood by – she had been fighting mental illness with Harrison most of his life and she didn't want to lose him to this illness. It seemed Harrison's mind drifted away to a dark place, seconds of hearing the news. It was more than he could take, so he simply became a third party to himself. The transformation was remarkable.

Lydia grabbed Harrison's elbow, "What can I do?" **"Nothing Lydia, nothing, my friend already took care of that."** Harrison said seriously.

"Mason, we must leave – we need to get Paris." Harrison said his goodbyes and told his family he loved them. Lydia asked Harrison to promise her that he would be okay – Harrison replied with, **"I have never promised you that Lydia, I have only ever promised you that I will do the best that I can and that is what I will do!"**

Harrison asked that I drive while he made a series of planning telephone calls. By the time we arrived to the airport, an hour drive, a Gulfstream jet was parked with the staircase down, waiting us. Four people dressed in uniform were waiting on us and Harrison went directly to the pilot and explained to him the situation. In the meantime the luggage was being loaded onto the jet. We boarded the jet and the pilot came to Harrison and assured him that the jet and their services were at his full disposal. Harrison responded to him with, **"You are a good man, sir, thank you!"**

I had not said anything to Harrison. I knew that he was in no place to be questioned or bothered. It was impossible to not notice that this man, Harrison, who was so filled with the "now" and the appreciation of everything around him; quickly became the corporate executive he once was in his early years, before the illness manifested. He was stealth in thought and purpose. Yet he was also consumed with pain.

The lavish jet propelled itself forward and built speed quickly. I recall feeling some anxiety, as the plane shuddered and then took off. We were airborne and banking within seconds towards New York City. As soon as the pilot cleared us to walk about the cabin, Harrison promptly moved to a desk area that had a telephone. Harrison was making a call to his concierge at his apartment on New York City's upper West Side.

"David, hello, Harrison Remy here. David, I need you to call my psychiatrist in the city and get me an appointment first thing tomorrow morning. My plans have changed. I will be in the city for the night only and heading directly to Paris tomorrow."

Harrison was intense. I was reminded about how structured Harrison must keep his environment. It was obvious that this was the last thing he wanted to do, but if he didn't, he too would succumb to the devastation brought on by his illness. He was acutely aware of this consequence and the situation. Harrison's drawn face, was enough to describe he was entering an emotional hell. I walked back to sit near him.

Chapter 24

Systems and Treatment

"Mason, do you have any idea how dreadful, difficult, demeaning and humiliating it is to try to get mental health needs when you have no money? It is insanity within itself. I have walked clear across cities to free clinics and social services to no avail. It is such a painful place to be, to find yourself slip into the abyss fully aware."

Harrison just stared out the window towards the clouds on the horizon.

"It isn't anger that I feel, it is more helplessness. The illness took Oliver's life, not Oliver. He was alone! I never wanted him or anyone else to be alone." Then silence came over the plane for the rest of the flight.

The aircraft started its descent and the pilot let us know that we must prepare for landing. The jet landed with a hard thud, as I finally became aware of how fast we were going. Soon the plane slowed and began to taxi to the tarmac. The jet opened to a set of stairs. We walked down the jet stairs and into a waiting car. We immediately left for the city. It was around 5 o'clock and the city was lit with holiday décor. Harrison pointed out this and that.

As the car pulled down central park west we stopped in front of a long awning where we were greeted by a doorman. We proceeded into the building an up the elevators to the 8th floor and through double doors into Harrison's New York apartment. It was beautiful, contemporary and very much Harrison Remy.

On the breakfast bar, there was a printed itinerary of Harrison's day for tomorrow. It consisted of the following things: a visit to the psychiatrist, psychologist and the pharmacy. Harrison reviewed the list, made a quick call to Ruthie to have her arrange for the dogs' trip to be delayed a couple of weeks and left in Ohio. He then retired to bed and asked me to go enjoy the city.

I chose to stay in the apartment to reflect and write, rather than run around New York during this difficult time. On the 11 o'clock news, I realized it had gone public about Oliver's death.

Chapter 25

New York City and onto Paris

The next day Harrison would be gone most of the day and I was busy in anticipation for Paris. When Harrison arrived back to the apartment, he looked as if he had aged considerably. Within hours we were being driven back to the airport and the same jet and crew for our departure to Paris. If it were not for the circumstances, this would have been an exciting time. Harrison was sensitive to the fact that I was not a world traveler and every once in a while would give me a comforting wink, to let me know that it was okay to be excited.

After dinner on the plane, we retired for the evening. I was awakened by the flight attendant when she said, "You might want to wake up. We are descending into Paris." Harrison had already been up and freshened up. It wasn't long before we were landing in Paris.

The air was chilly when the door opened to the aircraft. There was a large black sedan waiting for us and we went directly to the car while the luggage was being loaded into the trunk. Before getting into the car, Harrison approached the man driving and gave him a 'hello' in perfect French tradition with complete with a kiss on both cheeks. The driver, Frederic, said, "It is so good to have you here Harrison." Frederic was Oliver's butler and right hand man in Paris. His sense of loss was obvious. As we approached the gates, customs asked for our passports, glanced at them and motioned us on.

Around fifty minutes later, we pulled up to enormous gates. The gates opened and we pulled into a perfectly manicured European estate complete with fountains and sculptures. It was truly breathtaking. When I looked ahead, I realized that this was an actual mansion in every sense of the word. Harrison caught my jaw dropping… **"Oliver did very well for himself and despite what anyone might say about him, he knew that, he loved his life!"** and smiled.

As we emerged from the car, several house staff walked out of the two huge wooden doors. Each staff member had tears in his or her eyes. Once again, Harrison's remarkable ability to go from one emotion to the next unfolded as the corporate man transformed into a man whose tears ran like Seine River itself. He became grief-stricken in an instant. Like a grandfather, he comforted all of Oliver's faithful employees. When we stepped into the house, I realized that this place was nicer than any hotel I had ever seen in my life.

We all moved into the library where we sat and discussed everyone's well-being. Harrison was so concerned about all of them. It was Pascal, the estate manager that broke the silence about Oliver. Harrison rose slowly from his seat and addressed the room of people.

"Now listen closely because I will say it only once, Oliver died of a disease as serious as Cancer itself. There will be no blame, no 'what-ifs' and no guilt. He loved all of you and we will celebrate his life and not submerse ourselves in the pain of his death."

Chapter 26

Oliver and Suicide

Because of who he was, Harrison lifted the dense air in the room with his words. With the staff feeling more at ease, I enjoyed listening to memories of Oliver and his antics that generally included Harrison. Harrison and I then took a walk on the grounds. It was hard for me to conceive why anyone that lived like this and had such wonderful people around them would end their life. Yet I was also starting to understand the complexity of mental illness as well as the severity. Harrison started reminiscing.

"We used to have huge parties here at this house. Oliver and I would write short plays, comic and tragic and have friends perform them on the center balcony. Oliver enjoyed the eccentricity of it all and his wife enjoyed showing off. I... I just enjoyed the people. All walks of life would attend; artists and the literati along with the social elite. The parties were always very dignified and raised great sums of money for various mental health organizations. Oliver loved parties but wasn't particularly fond of people. He did enjoy entertaining and sharing with those close to him."

Harrison then left me to go do some work pertaining to Oliver's death. It was obvious the respect Oliver had for Harrison and how much he did rely on him. As strong as Harrison obviously was, I could not help but feel a great sense of sadness for his loss. He lost what was the equivalent to a younger brother and quite possibly a fellow soldier in a war against a disease.

That afternoon Harrison and I went into the city of Paris. The drive into the city was beautiful. Harrison told me to be sure to keep my eyes to the left as we entered the city of lights and before me appeared the Eiffel Tower in all its glory. We slowly cruised along the Seine to the West Bank. When we came upon a long barge that had been permanently docked, we got out of the car and walked the plank to one of the most beautiful restaurants I have ever seen. Harrison explained that this place once was not so well known, but under new ownership it had taken on a reputation as one of the best places to dine in Paris.

We must have had one of the best seats in the place, because no view was obstructed from some of the most beautiful landmarks of Paris. It is obvious that Harrison is very familiar with Paris and I ask him why that is.

"In one of my many careers, Paris was more like a second home for me. I spent a great deal of time here – nearly a week per month, actually. The city always had a certain allure to me since the first time I experienced it with my mother. I feel very at home in Paris as I do in many cities throughout the world."

"You certainly had some extraordinary careers didn't you?"

"When you mix the fearless with bipolar disorder, you are bound to get a very interesting life, Mason." Harrison says with a smile.

Harrison then looked at me as our wine was being poured and said, **"You know Mason, you can talk about Oliver and you can discuss how he died..."**

I was happy that Harrison had broken that conversation open because Oliver's death was definitely weighing on my mind, as was what Harrison's impression was. Harrison opened up about it immediately.

"Suicide… What a difficult thing for so many people to discuss. For one to understand the depths of this pain are impossible unless you have lived it, yet we live it differently even when we experience it."

Harrison became visually old again in front of my eyes, his heart seemed to sink and his eyes simply glossed over in pain. Even his shoulders lowered as he began to speak:

"Mason, it really isn't about suicide. It is the battle lost against an illness. I have heard so many people define suicide. They say it is a choice, or the person took their own life, or they were selfish and so forth. None of that is true. Just as anyone does with anything that can't be defined or 'answered back' – we make up our own definition, and I know this first hand.

When I lived in Denver after a great night out with friends, I got a call from the Denver police. My telephone number was found at the apartment of a dear friend of mine, Michael. The police were calling me to see if I knew him. I told them that I did know him and that he is a friend – they told me he was dead and hanging in his apartment as they were talking with me.

Michael was the same age as I. We were in our early twenties, both professionals and both a lot of fun. We were the 'in crowd' in Denver at the time. To be perfectly honest, I never even heard the words mental illness at that point in my life. I was stunned and in shock, completely. The officer kept talking and I just didn't have the ability to speak. Finally, I said – what do you want me to do? They wanted me to identify him, and a beautiful Saturday afternoon turned to solid darkness. I didn't know what to think after identifying Michael. The guy hanged himself. He was just with friends and me the night before and I was then staring at his dead body. I think every human emotion came over me all at the same time.

Obviously I had had suicidal tendencies by that time in my life, but I never thought of following through. Michael did and he did it with no question.

After speaking with all of our friends and they all came to my apartment, I really just wanted to be alone. I was tired of the speculation. I finally said, 'You know what? It doesn't matter why. He is dead!' I screamed it, I believe. They ran the gambit: Was he crazy? Was he doing something wrong, criminal and so on? I got fed up with it because the definition of Michael, just 12 hours before was this wonderful 22 year old man that was great looking and a lot of fun and our very friends were disparaging that definition.

I met his mother the next day for dinner as she flew in from Kansas. Michael had gone through many things in his life. He had "issues" and that is how she defined them to me. She never brought up mental illness. I drilled her for answers. Was he lying to us, as friends? Was he involved in something he shouldn't be? Surely there was something! She wasn't willing to give me any more than the fact Michael had, "issues".

I digress, there is no death that is more painful than another, but suicide is hard. One thing that always amazed me about suicide is that if you don't achieve it – you are vilified, if you do achieve it, you are memorialized or pitied. Does that really make any sense?

Suicide is not easy – I have attempted it many times and it will scare the hell out of you up to the point that it is too late. I am alive only by fate, not by determination or choice. Suicide, my friend is not a choice when it comes to mental illness, it a decision that is made for you by the illness that convinces you that the demons are all real. The choice that one has is to maintain a treatment plan to the absolute best of their ability. Upon death, things are out of all our control.

Furthermore, Mason – death is not the tragedy, having never lived is the tragedy and so many have never lived."

The entire next week was consumed by friends and family. An intimate memorial was held at Oliver's home in Paris and then his body would be flown back to the States for a more public memorial that Harrison would not attend.

Harrison and I prepared to get back to New York City. He had done all that he could personally do for the situation here.

Chapter 27

Back to New York City

Upon our return to New York, we walked
back into Harrison's apartment, there stood a man in his 60's but
looked as though he was in his 40's. He was a good looking
man, dressed well.

As Harrison came around the corner he yelled, **"JAKE!"** and
they embraced in one of those aggressive masculine locks. Jake
would be the closest thing to a son Harrison has. Jake and
Harrison met when Jake was only eighteen years old and was
sent to prison. He was a white-boy that was brought up in the
ghetto, because that is all his mother could afford. His mother
was addicted to crack cocaine and Jake was often passed from
one person to another. At one point he was "sold" by his own
grandparents. The two of them could not have a more different
upbringing.

Harrison always saw something in Jake and for one reason or
another, his heart attached to him in a fatherly way. Very slowly,
Jake got to a point where he trusted Harrison. Through the years,
Jake has had his ups and downs, especially his younger years
where he was learning about how life could be. He never
believed that life could be anything other than it was and that, for
him, was survival.

Today, he is educated in social work and runs the foundation
Harrison developed to address the mental health issues affecting
juveniles. Jake's firsthand experience of a turbulent, poverty
stricken life had lent its hand to the foundation on a level that not
even Harrison could have imagined.

There was a true trust that Harrison had in Jake and almost immediately without Jake even having to ask, Harrison emptied his heart about how difficult the past several days had been regarding Oliver's death.

Jake was a very proactive, understanding person and had Harrison go into the library and take a nap. Jake and I move into the kitchen.

It is obvious to me that Jake is very confident and very sincere. There is definitely something ornery about him. Jake starts the conversation:

"I am sorry that I couldn't be in Paris. Pa has to do some things on his own without the input and opinions of others."

The important thing was that Jake was here to help rebuild him after he gave everything of himself to Oliver's circumstances.

"I love the old goat, but he has always taken on far more responsibility for others than he needed to, that includes me." Jakes says with concern. This bond was obvious.

There was also an interesting difference between Harrison and Jake, one that surpassed their upbringing. Jake was somewhat of a womanizing flirt, but in a nice way. He was much flashier than Harrison – but much like Harrison, his core values were solid.

I looked out of the kitchen doors that open onto a balcony that overlooks Central Park and Jakes says:

"Impressive isn't it? I hated people that lived like this when I first met Harrison. I simply hated them. I didn't want to like Harrison, but Pa was the first person in my life that gave a shit. He is the first person that I ever cried in front of. I couldn't figure out who the hell this guy was because I never met anyone like him. He is kind of smart too," Jake says laughing: "But not street smart. He is dumb as a box of rocks when it comes to the streets!"

I asked, "What is the secret to the success of the foundation and its programs?"

"That is simple Mason, if you cannot get past yourself; you are not going to learn anything."

"That must be a hard thing to teach."

"Not as hard as you might think. There is always someone that has it worse than you and that example is usually a conduit to someone else's heart. Gratitude and respect do incredible things"

During the years where Harrison met his "lost", he realized a question that no one had asked many of the people that were homeless, incarcerated or in hospitals. That question was "why?" Of course the first response was generally an excuse, but then Harrison did something that most never did – he continued to ask "why?" Harrison found that by the time you get to the seventh why, you discovered the core to the issue that lead to the "now". Some would get to that core before the seventh why, but for most, it took that additional time and caring to ask in order to get to the core of what drives a person.

When you compound the issues of mental illness with generational poverty, abuse, loneliness, lack of education, entitlement and in general – people not caring – you find a person in a very difficult position. Then, when society does notice that person – it is often too late. They have acted out and been labeled.

Harrison despised this component of society and the human race. He learned that even when he sat in front a person that might have broken into twenty homes or a person so addicted to drugs that they behaved horribly – he could find that inner child and equate the emotional intelligence of that person.

Some called that a gift, Harrison called nothing more than caring enough to give another human being the time to talk unconditionally and discovering themselves.

"If you ever want to see Harrison angry, Mason – turn on the news and show him a man that did something horrible like shooting in a public building. But, it's not just any kind of shooting; a shooting in which the media deemed the shooter to be mentally ill. You'll see Harrison immediately research that person that did the act. You'll see Harrison find a history of psychiatric issues, incarcerations, schools and a court system that failed the shooter. You will see a man that was once a boy that was labeled and then thrown aside. That's not always the case and when it is not, Harrison will be the first to recognize it – but Harrison's fury will show when a crime like this happens. Not only is the person with the illness now dead – but innocent people are hurt or killed. Innocent people that should have never had to experience the wrath of a broken system," Jake says passionately

Harrison walks around the corner rubbing his eyes and Jakes yells out: "Well it is about time, you old yuppie!" However, Jake included several superlatives. Harrison looks at him and says, **"Why must you use that language?"**

"It gets the point across, Pa!"

"It shows a lack of vocabulary, son, that is what it shows!" as Harrison rolls his eyes.

Jake smiles, "He told me that the first day I met him in prison!" It is clear that Jake takes some liberties in annoying Harrison's more reserved personality.

"Mason, has Jake corrupted you yet?" Harrison says with an insincere voice. **"What plans have you made, Jake?"** Harrison says in a concerned tone I have heard only a few times before.

"Well, I was thinking…" Harrisons stops Jake, **"Oh my, he is thinking again!"** Jakes continues, "Anyway, a former foundation client is having an art exhibit in the village and I thought we would all go!"

"And what time does this start, Jake?"

"Well, I figure if we leave right now, we will be exactly one hour late!"

Harrison turns, looks at me, and heads to his bedroom to get ready, shaking his head along the way.

Twenty minutes later we meet in the foyer of the apartment. Harrison comes dressed in solid black Armani. Jake bumps against my shoulder and said: "Promise to shoot me if I ever dress like that!" Harrison turned and looked at Jake then me and says, **"Why wait?"** and we all started laughing.

When we pile into the town car, it seems the car is too small to confine all of Jake's energy. Harrison tells him to 'pipe down'. Along the drive, Jake is giving me a tour of all the fun stops in New York.

As we step out of the car to the red carpet laid out, several people do gasp. I am immediately brought to the reality that Harrison's vision is one of the reasons this artist is having an art show rather than a prison sentence. It was actually a bit overwhelming, however Harrison is not impressed with himself, and he believes that all individuals deserve the full ownership of their own success.

As we started our rounds in the gallery, Harrison simply allows himself to be completely consumed by the art. One of the first paintings Harrison saw echoed back at him like a voice across a canyon. The painting depicted a man looking over the world of the inner city, poverty and crime. Behind the man, is another world represented by strong buildings and solid foundations. Harrison was moved to tears and said, **"It is absolutely incredible what just a little love and respect can do for a person. There is no science to humanity; there is love and respect or hatred and judgment."** Harrison had a way of saying a lot with few words.

The artist introduced himself to Harrison, and personally thanked him. Harrison acknowledged the gratitude, however he said, **"It is I who thank you for your contribution to life!"**

We left the gallery in an upbeat mood and Jake insisted that we go to the old "White Horse" – a literati bar in the village. Harrison said, **"We will go for just an hour and then I am going home!"** Jake is happy with this compromise.

Walking in and sitting at the bar, I notice they are having a poetry reading and a man walks directly to Harrison and hands him a microphone and Harrison takes it without a second thought:

Shadows of Darkness
Mixed with beams of light
My soul reflects the color
Of the moods I withhold
Stumbling for the door
With outstretched hand
Not knowing what lies behind
As I open it all the more
Stepping into a room
Of maybe five or six
I see the doors of choice
Before me and my guests

Shall I think or just move
Jump or stand and wait
The selection is very important
Life changing this will make
To live with this choice
Is the consequence I shall take!

The bar was silent as Harrison handed the microphone back to
the young man. Without missing a beat, Jake leans over to
Harrison and says, "You just made that shit up didn't you?"
Harrison turns to him with a look of dismay but could not hold
back his laughter at Jake. **"Yes, Jake, I just made that shit
up!"** Jake looks at me, "Isn't that shit amazing – he should have
been a rapper!" Harrison just drops his head and laughs at the
same time saying, **"Unbelievable!"** In the meantime, I'm
laughing at this hysterically.

As I sat there and observed Harrison; I was once again reminded
of how Harrison could be in a moment and live in the now. He
flourished around artists of all kinds, yet he never considered
himself one of them, just an admirer, eager to learn and absorb.

We headed back to the apartment after the agreed one hour.

That evening, I sat and thought more about Harrison, Jake and all
that had just happened with Oliver. What goes through
Harrison's mind? Does he ever just sit back and say; "Wow, this
is my life?" He seems so content even when things are chaotic
around him. It is also very interesting how he accepts people for
who they are. He once said to me, "People are not their actions,
not their mistakes, you must look for their heart." Harrison not
only believed this, he lived it.

Chapter 28

Preparing for South Africa

After a couple of days in New York, Jake came and left often, much like the haunting of a ghost. Harrison finally said what Jake and I knew he was thinking.

"I know we haven't been in the city for as long I normally am, but given the circumstances of the past few weeks, I really need to get to South Africa."

Jake immediately says, "Well it is about time you fess up!" Harrison just grins at him.

That entire day was spent with Jake helping Harrison organize the trip that was taking place more than a month before it normally does. I think the city was just too much for Harrison at the time; it was too chaotic.

Harrison arranged for Lydia and her family to come to New York and stay at his apartment for as long as they wished even though he would not be there. I could tell that Harrison felt sad about not being able to share the city with Lydia and her family, but he really did need to get refueled and South Africa is where he found the most peace.

Jake worked at the same energy level in the same way he enjoyed life: anxious. He was working frantically to make this transition as smooth as possible. Jake knew Harrison very well and even though this was Harrison's decision, it involved a change of routine. Anytime there was a change in Harrison's routine, there was an opportunity for his illness to engage and thereby leaving

Harrison symptomatic. Given the recent circumstances, Jake was not taking any chances and I felt sorry for anyone who tried to make it difficult to get things done.

Everything from the dogs getting to South Africa, to our flight, to the people that take care of the plantation in South Africa being notified was happening all at once. Then, out of the blue, Jake said to Harrison, "Let's go!"

Jake was taking Harrison to Harrison's therapist and Jake was sitting in on the meeting. There was no way that Jake was allowing Harrison to leave the country until he was convinced that Harrison was stable. The other interesting factor was that Lydia was conference-called into the meeting and while Harrison was a man very much in control of his life – he would not be leaving for South Africa until Lydia and Jake said he could leave.

It was interesting that Harrison took these steps as a translation of love, and not a controlling factor. He once told me that he had an army around him to defend himself against mental illness and I was seeing that front line defense in action.

By the days end, everything had been arranged and Harrison was given the go ahead to head to his personal nirvana, South Africa. We would leave in the morning.

My anticipation left me sleepless. New York was one thing, Paris was another, and South Africa was not something I could even conceive. The excitement was building.

Chapter 29

Spirituality

Boarding a private jet, once again, was exciting for me. Harrison always chartered private jets – he would not fly commercial. One thing was different this time, however. After meeting several people in Harrison's life, I couldn't help but think how different it really is to live like Harrison does; compared to how he has lived. Once we got seated and comfortable, for what was going to be a very long flight, I decided that further exploration of that dichotomy would be my educational subject on this trip.

Harrison was visibly excited. The aircraft lifted off the ground and in front of my eyes, I swear that I saw years drip off of Harrison's face. I asked Harrison, "What is that?"

"What is what, Mason?"

"At times, it is as if years pile on and then melt off of your face. What is that?"

Harrison began to answer with a smirk, **"I guess it is stress. I also know that I have one of those faces and set of eyes that can't hide a damn thing. I was certainly never good at poker!"**

"Does your life in the States bring on that much stress?"

"No, it doesn't, not today. It's a hard thing to try to describe, but there has always been a weight that has been on my heart

ever since the dark days and leaving it all behind, sometimes just makes me feel better or lighter."

"Harrison, this life… you charter a jet, you live in wonderful homes, and you socialize with the who's who and the forgotten. You have been homeless; you have been rich; you have been imprisoned and then honored; everything always is in such contrast."

"Mason, that didn't start with the dark days – it has always been that way. My first flight on a private jet was when I was only 20 years old. My life has always been a conundrum of extremes. Gifted in many ways and cursed in others. The curse was mainly no sense of balance and a huge sense of self-destruction.

One of the many misrepresentations about me is the idea that I somehow think that I am entitled to a first class life and that I strive for luxury. That simply is not the case and it never has been.

Do I know the finer things in life when it comes to materials? Yes. Do I appreciate them? Yes. However, what people have never been able to identify with is that I was always on a mission to experience every aspect of this world I could. Some found vacations to Disneyland the best thing ever – I didn't. I never saw the world as a big place and if I wanted to see Eastern Europe, or Europe or Africa, India or anywhere else – I generally did.

Now what I did do that was wrong was go about it the wrong way a few times. But to look at me and judge me based on the fact that I see the world for myself versus sitting in a sofa and watching it go by through a television screen is not an argument I will ever entertain.

"How did you find your way out of that conundrum?"

"Slowly, very slowly! It has taken years to find balance and even to this day, I sometimes lose sight of it. However, what I find sad in those that simply give up against the mental illnesses- and I don't mean suicide- is that we all have to take the good with the bad. At times life is all we hoped it would be and at other times it is everything we wished it weren't. I haven't met many people at all, mentally ill or not that don't have this issue with life. I also believe that if anyone were to be ostracized that their bad days would be just as bad as some of mine. Having people in your life and allowing people to love you is very important to the human spirit, not just the mentally ill.

One of the differences between a person without a mental illness and the person with a mental illness is the response to circumstances and situations. My response most likely will not be the same as yours because my first instinct is going to be a bit irrational or illogical. This does not, however, mean that your point of view is more correct than mine, it simply means I will have a much more impulsive response."

"I have to admit Harrison, that I find mental illness very confusing."

"YOU? Try living with it and not being able to get rid of it!" Harrison said with a shrug.

"Mason, mental illness can be a real bitch, to put it bluntly. However, we who have a mental illness might not have a choice in some things, we do have a choice as to whether we treat it or not. I have explored all options personally and I am here to tell you, following any treatment plan is better than no treatment plan at all.

Here is another aspect of mental illness. With cancer, you have a person that is diagnosed. Everyone is on board to find the best treatment and love and support one another. With mental illness, you often times have someone kicking and screaming to not get treatment.

You might ask, 'Why would someone not want to be treated?' Well, take this into account: There have been many times that I have been so medicated I didn't even have a personality. Can you imagine me without a personality? I simply laid there and stared. At one point in my life I came very close to going into a catatonic state, I had given up completely. The mind is the single most important organ in the body, yet when it is sick, it is the least understood and I assure you, mental illness is often the last illness to get any compassion.

People are constantly judging so many with mental illness because so many have addiction issues or they run away or whatever else. I challenge anyone on this earth to walk a day in the mind of someone that is mentally ill and see how long they last before they will take anything available to them to escape those demons... ANYONE! If you have cancer, they give you morphine to escape the pain. If you have mental illness you are given medications, however it can take up to a month before you feel the effects! I have never blamed a person for turning to drugs or alcohol. Now, with that said, it is not the right choice, it worsens everything. But exactly how do you touch the core of the problem if your first response is criticism and judgment? I have said to so many that have addiction issues and are in crisis... "I get it, you drank that bottle of vodka, you numbed yourself, however... you well know that when that vodka wears off you are going to be in a dangerous state, so will you allow me to help you before that happens." I assure you that works much better than, 'You are a freakin' loser and a drunk!' Same goes for drugs. Come on, does anyone truly like to feel horrible?

Just think of the facts. If you go screaming at someone that has schizophrenia and is high on something... someone is going to get hurt. This is why crisis intervention with law enforcement is so very important. Far too many have met very sad fates at the hand of not being educated in mental illness."

"Harrison, how in the hell do you keep this all straight in your mind when it pertains to your own life? You have run the gambit with all these symptoms."

"Life is not nearly as complex as I thought it once was, Mason. I don't have to be rich or poor, I don't have to be successful or a failure, I don't have to be good looking or ugly. I am not one of those people. They exist... I know many of them. I am not one of them. I am all of it. I am just me. People can take it or leave it and I assure you many have left it. No one is entitled to anything in this life; we are all just instruments in it. We can all be the best that we can be!

"They say to never discuss religion with anyone, do subscribe to this rule?"

Harrison starts laughing, "No, I don't subscribe to that rule and here is why, a majority of people base their whole character on religion and politics and I would much rather define my own than have someone define it for me."

"Then I guess I will bring up religion first! What is your religion?"

"I was brought up Catholic and I am happy that I was. I am a Christian and I am human. I don't hate many things in the world. I can't stand a hypocrite. I know many wonderful Catholic people, I grew up with them. Most of my family is Catholic. However, I don't believe in the entire dogma of Catholicism, so how could I belong to the church? That would make me a hypocrite. It is not an insult to Catholicism by any means. I just think it would be more insulting for me to walk into a Catholic church and accept communion when I don't agree with the entire dogma.

To be perfectly frank, I have found inspiration in nearly every religion there is and the very inspiration I have found through those examples of the people from all of those religions are my proof of God. I have Muslim friends, Jewish friends, Hindu and Buddhist friends; hell, I even have atheist friends.

If there is one thing I know about God it is this, I would much rather stand before him as a sinner, a liar and a thief than I would ever want to stand before him as someone that assumed his job of judging someone else. I will leave that to the big guy."

"So, do you subscribe to any dogma within Christianity?"

"No. God is in people and he makes himself known quite clearly all the time if you just listen. During the dark years, people came out of the woodwork for my family and I, they brought love even if they had no understanding; they brought love. They visited me in jail and prison. Mind you, these are people that would never be placed in a situation of knowing someone who was in prison, let alone visiting them. That is God!

Then there were those that were supposed to be close to my family, were family and I've never seen them once. Not even a letter and never have. That is not God; that is judgment.

Faith is a funny thing, I guess. When you really have faith, you live it so you really aren't that guarded about your own person and your own life. There are people that think they are very faithful because they don't lie, cheat or steal. Well, I always liked the verse in the Bible: Mathew 25:34 that discusses, 'when did we feed you, when did we visit you in prison and so on. You did it when you were there for the least of my brothers.' I don't worry about being hurt by others simply because they are in need and in a bad place in their lives. If I were to worry at all about anyone, I would be worried about those that use the word, "faith" and don't live it. Now that is something I find dangerous and pathetic.

The bottom line Mason is the fact that I am very spiritual, I am a Christian but I do not limit God in my life by confining him to a certain system. That, for me is contradictory. Through God all things are possible – I actually believe that, in fact, I know it. The best thing I can do is be an example of it to the best of my ability, however, I am not God so I stumble and fall all the time – but I always find it interesting and rewarding when I trip over something and realize it was there for a reason.

When I was first diagnosed with bipolar disorder, God was the first thing I thought of. You can't see him, you can't feel him, taste, or smell him, but he is real. Same goes with mental illness. It was affecting my life along with everyone around me. Now how do you prove something like that? I wasn't going to spend my life trying to prove it. I decided to utilize it and celebrate it, just like I do God."

Harrison's interpretation of God made a lot of sense to me. I am from a devout Catholic family so some things seem a little 'new age' for me to conceive – but at the core of Harrison's belief system is love and I guess it would be difficult to go wrong with that.

After hours on this subject, it was time to get some rest prior to landing in Johannesburg, which was still eight hours away.

Chapter 30

Arriving in South Africa

I was not fully awake as we were walking down the stairs. A car was waiting on the tarmac for us, and we loaded our belongings into the trunk. When we were all loaded up, the car left. As we drove out of the airport, I looked over at Harrison.

I looked into his eyes and saw that the hurt and stillness were erased. His eyes looked alive. He looked alive. It was almost as though this place turned time backwards, and revived the dead parts of his soul. I'm sure that somewhere, deep in the cavernous space that was the soul, Harrison was still grieving Oliver. But in the South African sun, if only for a moment, it was erased.

It was still summer in South Africa and the temperature was rising. I wanted to perform some kind of test or experiment to see if this was real. Ever since I got the assignment to follow Harrison for a year, I had been to so many places and met so many people. It almost seemed like a dream, but I remind myself daily that it's reality. I can't believe I just flew over the equator! Nearly two hours north of Johannesburg, we pulled up to two beautiful iron gates. Harrison got out of the car and entered a code into a box with a keypad. The gates opened. When Harrison jumped back into the car he exclaimed: **"We are home!"**

On both sides of road is "the bush", a term used for the wild places in South Africa. Harrison told me to keep my eyes open as 'you never know what you might see'. I then realized, I am not in a zoo, I am in the bush of South Africa!

We drove for two more miles and came upon another gate. This one is covered with greenery and seems to be much more about security than it looks. As the gate opens, my eyes widen in disbelief.

Lush green grass, several beautiful buildings, fountains and a big house were before me. The largest house that I saw made the other homes Harrison had seem humble. It isn't like Oliver's elegant mansion outside of Paris. The house is elegant too, but of a different style. As a writer, words are very important, and I don't think I can call this place a house. No, the correct word for this place is an estate. It's huge and there are several beautiful homes that I can see on the property.

The car pulls up to the circular drive around the fountain that has a metal elephant blowing water over metal baby elephants; and a metal gazelle leaping through the water.

Harrison can't even wait for the car to stop before opening the door. Several people emerge from the house in traditional South African garments.

Harrison galloped up the stairs onto the porch and hugged everyone as I followed and we headed into the main entry hall. It was quite a welcoming committee and Harrison was moved to tears in the moment.

Harrison introduces me. There was Moda, a beautiful dark skinned woman with perfect complexion, her husband, Lepe; Mana their daughter; and Len, their son. This was the Odo family and they run the home. It is quite clear that Harrison considers them all family.

The exterior of the main house is a white wash stone in Georgian Colonial Style. There are massive patios everywhere that span the entire perimeter of the house. Large fences surround the property, and the landscaping of the estate itself is done in the traditional South African style. The estate encompasses ten acres of land.

There are several bungalows on the property as well, that family and friends occupy during visits to the estate. Harrison considered this his home. At first, his parents were not sure whether they would like it or not. But after visiting the first time, they came to the estate every chance they could. Harrison's mother enjoyed Sun City and traveling by train down to Cape Town where the shopping was abundant. Harrison's dad loved the east coast along the Indian Ocean as well as the many national game reserves. Harrison once said his dad could leave at 5 'o clock in the morning and not come back until 5 'o clock in the afternoon, spending the day just driving around looking for animals.

Generally, his parents made the home their base and would take off throughout the country on week long trips.

As we all migrated to the large balcony off the kitchen overlooking a pool, we sat down at a table and Harrison started reminiscing.

Chapter 31

Harrison Reminiscing

Harrison starts:

"One year my parents decided they wanted to take their first cruise and it would be from New York to Cape Town. I never saw two people so happy to disembark a ship in my life. I guess being confined to the same activities for nearly two months nearly drove them out of their mind. At one point mom was willing to pay any price to fly from one of the ports to Cape Town, but dad said that was just ridiculous, even though he was ready to end the cruising experience himself.

When I asked my mother what she thought about cruising, she said it was like being canned tuna. Mom and Dad were not people who enjoyed being waited on. It took them both two weeks to recover and I never saw so much work completed at this house in my life. Trapping my mother for even a short amount of time was hard to do, she had nearly two months of energy bottled up and the first two weeks they were at this house she was a tornado of energy."

Harrison got up to use the restroom. Moda looked at me and said, "Harrison's parents were amazing people. The bond between the three of them was extraordinary and the sense of respect that had for one another was a true treasure.

When Harrison returned, he said, **"We have to get settled and rested up from this long day of travel!"** So we all went to our respective rooms to unpack and unwind.

All bedrooms were on the second floor and were connected by a large balcony. While unpacking, I heard a thunderous blast. I rushed to the balcony. Through all the welcoming, I had nearly forgotten that I was in the middle of the African bush. What I saw brought so much excitement, my eyes were watering. A herd of elephants had come to the watering tanks.

They were splashing and spraying each other. I felt like a child again, with the same innocence and belief. I felt like I would have felt at five, if I ever saw in person my favorite dinosaur: the Tyrannosaurus Rex. Dinosaurs were mythical creatures, but the elephants had that same aura. I was excited to see them.

Down the way on the balcony I saw Harrison and heard him yelling: **"Hello"** to the elephant family. He knew each of their names. It wasn't long before herds of zebra and wildebeest along with gazelles came to visit. It was as if the bush had come to welcome Harrison home. He couldn't be more excited.

It came to mind that the reason that Harrison had so much in life was because that he enjoys everything in life.

Chapter 32

The Meaning of South Africa

Harrison and I sat down and watched the wildlife. I asked him about South Africa:

"Harrison, you have a strong connection with South Africa. Where does that come from?"

"Ah, South Africa, my soulful home! The first time I landed in Johannesburg, South Africa, at the age of 24 I had an overwhelming sense of belonging. Before I even left the airport I felt I was somehow home. That was internal however – getting out of the airport was very unfamiliar and somewhat hilarious. I had done NO research on South Africa before coming, so when I walked out to get into my rental car I was surprised when I sat down in the driver's seat and there was no steering wheel! The driver's side was on the right side of the car. Johannesburg airport is nearly downtown and I had never driven on the right side. I thought to myself, well, this is going be interesting and it certainly was! Horns were blowing at me left and right and I had no idea what was left or right at that point. It was comical, really.

By the time I got out of the city and the sheer fear and exhilaration of my driving adventure in Johannesburg, that feeling or sense of home was coming back to me. I was just amazed at the feeling of comfort that I had in this foreign country. I had been to many countries and never had this sense of belonging. Originally, I was excited about Cape Town, Pretoria, Durban and Sun City – I quickly realized

over the course of the trip that I was drawn towards the bush rather than the cities. It was the game reserves like Sabi Sabi and Krueger that I wanted to be. That surprised me a little, because I am not really an outdoors kind of a person.

Looking back, I was certainly manic at the time, at least hypo-manic. I could not get enough of each day. Everything meant something to me. The animals put me in a complete sense of wonder – even tears, just observing them. This was before the Lion King ever came out, but you could almost hear the score to it when you looked out on the bush. Sitting on the patio of the hotel room with a glass of wine and the sun setting while seeing the giraffe, elephant, zebra and wildebeest in their natural state was just amazing, no actually amazing doesn't give it justice, it was spiritually breathtaking.

Remember when I told you that sometimes you have to go back in your mind and memory and find a moment that gave you an immense amount of peace - A moment that gave you spiritual soundness? South Africa gave me a lot of those moments that I will treasure the rest of my life.

I remember when I came back from that trip which included Botswana and Zimbabwe as well. I visited my hometown and my parents had a little get together for my visit. We showed my video tape; yes, we only had video tapes back then, I was standing behind a relative and I heard her say to the person next to her, 'why would anyone want to go there?' Now at that age, 24 years, I was very different than I was at 34 years, let alone now. I was appalled! I thought to myself, "how simpleminded is that?" I didn't understand objectivity then – I was just as simple minded as she was. I was thinking my experience was the most important thing in the world and she was thinking her world was the only place to be. I was just as ignorant as she was, really.

There are 6.5 billion people on this earth and every single one of us is different. That is pretty amazing if you really stop and think about it. It takes all these differences. We need to be challenged and confronted in order to evolve and grow in every way, spiritually, physically, and intellectually and so on. Often times we don't realize that we are learning from the people that we may think are simple-minded.

For some, they get that sense of peace and joy from looking at their children and seeing their faces and their spouse's faces in them. They could not imagine not having children and experiencing that part of life. For me, if I were to wake up and find myself married with kids, living in the suburbs – I would have a heart attack! And they might have a heart attack if they were in the bush of South Africa and seeing a lion coming towards their buggy! There is no right or wrong to either one of these scenarios. Where the wrong comes in, is when we are not open minded enough and aware enough to experience others experiences through their eyes without judgment or prejudice. I have relatives that have children as you have met. I spend more time observing the parents than I do the children because through that observation I can get a grasp of the emotions that their family brings to them. If I were judgmental or prejudicial, which I have been at times, I would miss out on that and I would miss out on the wonders of diversity and the celebration of the differences among us all – therefore neglecting the opportunity to learn and grow.

South Africa, for me, teaches me the "Circle of Life" just like sons and daughters and grandchildren brings the "Circle of Life" to others.

Prejudice and ignorance, Mason – is a loss to the person that has it – not the learning tool for the person you are prejudice against. You will know you have come a long way when you look at someone you consider simple minded and realize you can learn from them, and there is no such thing as a simple minded person – just someone different than you and there are 6.5 billion others different than you!"

It was easy to understand how Harrison related life as a whole to the South African bush. Looking out to the wildlife that were grazing and watering in front of us, one could only see how different we all are, yet we and everything else in life is contingent on everything.

Chapter 33

Harrison on Judgment

Harrison continues discussing his perception of judgment:

"We need to be very careful when we are judging others – if we judge them at all. It is a very dangerous game that one plays with the heart of another. It has been my experience, in life, that those that are judging don't have the perception or intuition necessary to make an opinion, much less judge someone.

It is natural for us, as human beings to judge or have an opinion – but it is very important what motivates the judgment or opinion. Are we analyzing for education, to be informed or to just make ourselves feel better at the detriment of someone else and their ways?

More times than not – if you take the time to study your own judgment – you will find that it is either diversion or transference. Meaning you are diverting the things you might not like about yourself or the things you wish you had or were.

I have judged others and many times I was wrong. There have been many times that my perception of someone was right, but I decided that I owe them the right to prove that... yes, I have gotten hurt by this – but I have also learned so much by opening that door. I have found that in my decision to allow them to prove themselves, I gave myself a tremendous gift; a gift of education, understanding and compassion.

I have also been judged and know firsthand how disturbing it is to have someone decide what you are about and what you are thinking without your input. More times than not, if not always – they are wrong. You then find yourself in a position of using your energy to prove you are not what they say or think. It took a lot of years to realize that this is a massive waste of energy.

It is impossible to know the path a person has walked unless you ask them. It is careless and ignorant to make an opinion or judgment without knowing how hard their road has been. With this is mind, if you don't care enough to learn the experience of another, to understand why they are the way they are or have done what they have done; keep your opinions to yourself. Your judgment is uninformed and uneducated, therefore null and void. It is useless and only hurtful."

Speaking with Harrison or listening to him, always reminds me of how he felt judged by others. I ask him if there has ever been a time that he didn't feel judged.

"You know when you really find out how loved you are or how great humanity can be, is when you go through a very dark time. I take very little credit for the fact that I have had a successful recovery with mental illness. There have been so many people in my life that have shown me great diligence of love and respect. There have been people that have found something in me worth life when I couldn't find it myself.

These people had infused oxygen back into my lungs and love back into my heart. Throughout my life I have always had the privilege of meeting good people. Some I have hurt, some I have helped, a great deal of them I have disappointed at one time or another. Doctors, therapists, family, friends, and colleagues have simply mystified in me in their emotional generosity. I am very grateful for them and I am grateful for the fact that when I think about life and people, I have them to compare it all against.

I have told you before, Mason; it takes an army to keep me healthy. I have one hell of an army and I am deeply blessed by that.

It is also important to understand that many have tried to help me throughout the years. I have had friends go far beyond the call of duty to try to help me even after they knew of my mental illness. When I look back and ask myself why I didn't take that help, the only thing I can come up with, truly – is that none of us truly understood what I was dealing with. That includes me. My friends made an effort to understand and help me regain sanity and I just didn't receive it well. That was very disappointing to all of us and I lost a great deal of wonderful friends because of it.

"I heard you say that with great gifts comes great responsibility. Is that why you dedicated your life to the cause of mental health awareness?"

"In a word, yes. However, it is much more than just mental health awareness. We, as the mentally ill, are our own worst enemies so much of the time. That always bothered me. There are plenty of people with mental illness that you will never hear about because it can be hidden to a point if you have the resources to get the help that you need and if you have the support that you need.

What I saw, after being homeless, incarcerated, hospitalized and in shelters, was something that I couldn't conceive – yet it was so real. Even at the worst of my times, I was so much better off than most I met.

It truly broke my heart to see people battling the same illness that I did. However, on top of the illness, they battled a childhood of abuse, poverty and a true sense of hopelessness. I couldn't tolerate that, it sickened me. I saw that in Jake.

So many people in this world that are living in poverty, especially generational poverty and are hungry, uneducated and simply trying to survive have no voice in the world.

They don't have a voice because no one wants to deal with their issues. I've sat down with hundreds if not thousands of people that have been in circumstances that I could not fathom.

When I finally came home, I knew one thing and that was that I did have a voice and I knew how to use it. I also had a very thick layer of skin and a determination that was, shall we say, formidable. I will tell you one thing, Mason. I would much more fear any human being more than I would fear any one of those animals in the bush. If I were to fear anything, that is," Harrison finishes his lesson, and then winks. He winks as if he let me in on a big secret. That's the one thing I've learned about Harrison; his life is an open book, provided anyone takes the time to listen.

Harrison and I continued to talk about the animals and how much he enjoyed the sight of them. He had a connection to this land and country that I had not noticed he had in his other homes. While he was very close to the Michigan house that was very much his tie to his parents. New York City was his fun place.

South Africa was Harrison's home and he truly felt he could be himself here.

Chapter 34

Harrison and the Lion

Over the next couple of weeks, I had the privilege to experience South Africa. I enjoyed the safaris and the shopping and all that this great land had to offer. It was truly a dream come true. My evenings were filled with writing and making notes, trying to get the best understanding of Harrison Remy possible.

While sitting out on the balcony one morning, I had to review for a moment. I was reminded of several things. Harrison was in his 80th year. He had lived through mental hospitals, prison, more mental hospitals, suicide attempts, and hopelessness. He has been hated and loved; hungry and full; rich and poor; successful and defeated. Harrison has experienced being lost and then found; being beaten and then experiencing the exhilaration of triumph. How in the hell has he survived, let alone flourished? What drives him? I am only 22 years old and I am determined to understand this very thing. Every successful person is a beacon of light, and I want to discover the fire that is Harrison's light,

It was time to stop thinking and put down my coffee and head to the shower. I was to meet Harrison this morning and go on a safari with him to Palensburg National Park.

At the bottom of the stairs, I see Harrison, perfectly dressed. He is dressed head to toe in safari gear. Mrs. Odo was busy packing a cooler, and fueling the Safari Jeep. Harrison was cleaning his binoculars.

Mr. Odo approaches with the jeep and tells us we're all set to go. Mrs. Odo closes the cooler. Harrison and I each grab a handle on the cooler and head to the jeep. We were on our way.

Harrison handed me my own set of binoculars and a camera.

"You can keep that camera, Mason – I don't even know how to turn it on!"

As we started the car, it seemed as though Harrison was turning into an adventurous kid. The first set of gates opened and we had to wait on a herd of zebras and wildebeests to pass in front of us. Harrison was laughing at the little cows and colts woven in the heard. I knew once we got out of the main gate and onto the paved road it was going to be a hot and fun day in South Africa. The excitement was building along with the intense heat of the sun. The drive was fairly quick, only twenty minutes or so.

As we pulled into the park, I could not help notice that the rangers' jeeps had large guns on them. It was a reminder that this was not an American zoo.

Harrison pulled over close to a watering hole and I could not figure out why or what he was looking at so intensely. I followed his eyes and to my shock all I could see is the enormous mouth of a hippopotamus! Harrison just laughed as we pulled away. Over a little bridge, he stopped once again. There were more crocodiles than I had ever seen in my life basking in the sun along the banks of a very dry river. I am hollering like a little kid and Harrison is just laughing and laughing as he continues to drive forward knowing exactly what he is doing.

A couple other jeeps were pulled over on the side of the road and we pulled up into the mix. Obviously they spotted something. Although when I looked ahead it was a large pack of wild dogs and hyenas!

"They are dreadful creatures!" Harrison said as he laid on the horn to make them move.

Herds of zebra were everywhere and the golden landscape was breathtaking as we started to climb in elevation. As Harrison pulled to the side again, my jaw dropped as I saw a giraffe standing just feet away from us eating leaves off the top of a tree!

"Aren't they funny looking and beautiful all at the same time?" Harrison said giggling.

Further ahead was a large pavilion. Harrison said we would stop there and have a snack and some much needed water. As we opened the cooler, I couldn't believe all the goodies that Mrs. Odo had fixed for us to enjoy on this beautiful day. I was simply in awe as I thought about the entire day thus far. It was like a timeless milestone in my life, as though I had reached a new peak, felt the warmth of friends, and the experienced joy of discovery.

As we have our snack and water, Harrison describes the park and its history. He knows everything; even the animal population. He makes it a point to know all he can know about everything surrounding him. It's fascinating. He says it's something he learned from his maternal grandmother.

His gaze shifted to the right. I followed his stare to find, a massive male lion, nearly camouflaged, in the distance. The lion was slowly walking towards us. We quickly grab our binoculars. The size of this cat was seemed larger than any picture I'd ever seen. His stride and presence were powerful. It was undeniable why the world thinks of lions as kings of the jungle.

Harrison began talking:

"The lion resembles so much of what we strive to be. Wisdom exudes from its being, not his mouth. Power exudes from its presence, not his force. He is slow, steady, stable and secure in every step he takes. The lion is painfully aware of every motion in its environment at all times. He can and will walk by prey if he is not hungry, knowing it is unnecessary to kill for no reason. He knows full well he is taken care of and will be provided for. Intensely loyal, the lion puts up with no nonsense of threat to his family. It is simply unwise to tempt this loyalty and his eyes let you know this, but his roar will drive the point home!"

We continue to watch as the lion takes one secure step after another. The awe of seeing the lion in its natural environment was enhanced by Harrison's words. Harrison takes every example of nature to not only prove but guide a person to understanding. He helps everyone understand the whole, as he calls it: universe.

"We are all a part of this condition, Mason. Every action provokes a reaction from something or someone. Every action has a consequence or a reward. We are all responsible for this and responsible for our decisions as it affects everyone, absolutely everyone and everything thing.

When we have made wrong choices and decisions we are given circumstances that give us the opportunity to right our wrongs and learn. If we choose to ignore that opportunity, the process will repeat until we realize and act upon the opportunity. This is why ignorance is the most dangerous action of a human being – it puts us all back a step when we ignore. It stops progression, the link to the next step. Each and every one of us is the most important piece to the universe. Because of that, we are all one."

As I am looking through the binoculars at this majestic lion, I am listening to Harrison's words as if they are coming from the lion itself.

All the sudden Harrison says, **"PHEW that's some deep shit!"** and starts laughing!

I said, "Did you mean it?"

"Every word of it, but Mason you can't stay deep for too long, you will drown!" Harrison said with a very secure smirk and then a comforting wink.

Chapter 35

Balance

I had been taken in by Harrison's words and I wasn't willing to stop this conversation.

"Harrison, you talk about this balance but what about how you were hurt? For example, the people that assaulted you in prison. What is that balance and what did they learn or could they have learned? What could you learn from that?" They deserve to be hurt!"

"NO, Mason, they do not! You are foolish to think that they learned nothing. Regardless of what my spirit and body hurt, that was not the perception I gave them. I held my head up high each and every day. I did not succumb to becoming them! What they saw was someone that remained unchanged or even emotionally stronger. I gave them proof of something they wanted and couldn't even define, it wasn't my body; it was faith, confidence and oneness. Every one of them was put on that journey of that undefined part of me.

As the lion keeps balance in the universe, we must do the same. No matter what avenues we take, we cannot override the lessons the universe is determined to teach us. We must learn to be humbled and trustworthy of this.

You will never reach a peace and understanding until you can pray at night knowing, not believing, but knowing you could walk through flames the next day if you must when it is for the higher purpose in life and know that it will be okay."

By this time, I had a headache and I would have to think about all that Harrison had shared throughout the day, in order to garner the true meaning of Harrison's wisdom. We headed back to the house to relax and take some time for ourselves.

Chapter 36

Animals in the Wild and Homelessness

For me, the entire time in South Africa had been an adventure I would forever remember. I could not discount the lessons and history of Harrison. I spent a moment reflecting on Harrison's secret.

The more I learned about the man, the more I realized that it was the key. I'd discovered so much about Harrison, but I felt I could go on a journey for another year, and still not know the man as deeply as I wanted to. He was truly special, because he made everyone feel special. But I was determined to figure out Harrison's secret before we left South Africa. So much had been written about the man, but in my book, I wanted to add something new to the conversation, something everyone had missed, but was there all along. I didn't know if he would reveal it himself, or if I would have to ask; all I knew was I had to know it.

I believe that during my trip I was seeing Harrison at his best. He planned activities for us to do every single day, even if it was just swimming. Not only did we have plenty to do; each activity was an event. It wouldn't be long before we would be heading back to the States. I wasn't sure where we would be going, but I assumed it was back to New York.

I saw Harrison sitting out on the balcony and thought I would ask him if he minded my company for a bit. He said with a big smile, **"I would appreciate your company, Mason!"**

"Are you sad to see another year go by, Harrison?"

"Not really. I am grateful for every moment I get and with everything, comes passing. That is something I truly learned to appreciate – you must enjoy the now, young man!"

"There have been several moments in your life that I am sure you couldn't wait for the moment to pass, haven't there?"

"That is probably an understatement." Harrison says with a grin.

"So, what was the worst?"

"Homelessness! I think homelessness is the worst. Those were times that just weren't good all the way around. I don't like being hungry. There was no way to get help medically or mentally and it just seemed to be an abyss that I didn't know if I was going to get out of. I didn't like that."

"You always tell me that we learn from everything. What did you learn?"

"What aloneness was or is. That feeling never escaped me. There is a strange desperation, but not much you can do about it. You don't want to reach out to anyone even if they are there, but then again, if you don't you're going to die. People should not be homeless in the United States or anywhere for that matter and that is all there is to it. I know that some choose to be, supposedly anyway, but it just is not a 'God' thing to me. I think Mason, you might have even stumped me on that question because it is very difficult to describe in words just what that feels like. It connects and stabs nearly every part of you."

"Harrison, what do you think about it all, really?"

"About life?"

"Yeah, about life"

"I think it is amazing. Life, Mason is not the journey that you take; it is the collection of journeys you take by yourself and with others. What have you learned in these past several months, Mason?"

I really had to take a deep breath before answering Harrison. He just looked at me with a peaceful sigh and I said:

"I learned that I was to set out to meet a man that conquered mental illness, but that is not who I met."

"And who did you meet Mason?"

"I met you."

"Who did you think you were going to meet?"

"Your mental illness!"

Harrison slowly dropped his head and closed his eyes for a moment then looked back up at me with a tear in his eye and said,

"Well Mason, you learned the single most important thing about helping people with mental illness! They are not their illness, they have an illness."

Chapter 37

Self-Pity

The last week in South Africa was not as busy as I might have thought. We spent more time talking with the Odo family than anything else. Harrison really did feel as though they were just as much family as anyone else.

No one showed up this year to the South Africa home and while I do think Harrison hoped someone would, he also realized the journey was long for any of his aging relatives. It was then that I asked Harrison about self-pity.

"Oh, that is a nasty thing and I have indulged in it so many times. Self-pity, Mason is nothing but an excuse in life and there is no bigger lie than an excuse. One cannot do anything with an excuse, a reason, you can do something with – but not an excuse.

Even after I learned this concept, I still struggled with self-pity. One of the first things that I had to do was realize my faults and my mistakes in life regardless of how or why they happened. Once I was honest with myself about who I was, I could begin a journey of forgiving myself.

This is an interesting process. It made me realize the illusion of life was not my life. I was not taking ownership of my life, because how I had lived had been at the hands of the impulsive choices that I had made.

Yes, many things were initiated by my illness, however if that was the case, then I had to take ownership of my illness.

While mental illness is extremely difficult to deal with and control, it was my responsibility whether I liked it or not. It did not matter how people responded to my illness, it mattered how I responded to my illness.

For many years, I said to myself, 'If no one else believes that I have an illness, why should I?' The only person that hurt was me. With that frame of mind, I was living up to every negative stereotype of mental illness and thereby worsening everyone's perception of mental illness.

There is not one thing that I can think of that is good about self-pity. It is damaging all the way around. What I will say is that it is a process. Once you have been beaten down so far, either by your own mind or others, you inevitably get to a place that you simply just feel sorry for the person that is you.

I think for many people, this journey or facet of recovery starts in different ways. The way that it started for me was when I felt the illness was acknowledged and separated from my character. My parents and I had a saying in our house, 'we trust Harrison, but we do not trust the illness.' This was a very realistic way to deal with the beginning stages of recovery. It opened the door for me to say, 'Then let's stop the progression of the illness.' And not feel hated because I had it."

The days left in South Africa were peaceful and Harrison told me we would be flying back to New York to spend some more time with Jake and get an update on all that is going on with the foundation.

The boys never did make it to South Africa this year. Instead they went back to Michigan to stay with Ruthie. There were problems with the process and Harrison decided that it would be better for them to simply be in the great north of Michigan. I could tell Harrison missed them.

I had probably learned more about Harrison and his philosophy about life in South Africa than any other place and could have stayed an additional six months. When I told Harrison this he said: "The world keeps moving and so must we!"

We were then off to Johannesburg and back on to the aircraft for a very long flight back to the city. It would take us a few days to simply recover from the trip.

It was nice to back in the city, but what a change of pace from the African bush to the concrete jungle. I never got a chance in South Africa to ask Harrison to reveal his secret. I suppose I feel apprehensive about asking such a powerful man to reveal the trying tales of his heart. But I still can't get beyond seeing Harrison as anything less than a legend. That, I think, is a problem that I must get past, if I'm ever to finish my book.

Chapter 38

The Ultimate Change in Life

Having settled in to New York after our adventure in South Africa, we spent the first few days back in New York recovering from our trip. Today was Harrison's birthday. For the first time since we returned from South Africa, Harrison woke up at 9 o' clock in the morning, and got started on the day.

I met him for coffee at the breakfast bar.

"Good morning Harrison and happy birthday!"

"Thank you Mason. It's good to celebrate another year of life. When you get to be as old as me you thank God for every day you went out and *did* something, and didn't let it go to waste. In this, the twilight of my life, I'm happy for what I've been able to accomplish. I cannot say I wasted my life."

"And you haven't! You've done so well," I say, but notice a strange look come across Harrison's face. It looks like he's in pain.

"My chest hurts. It's probably nothing, I had a perfect EKG the last time I went to the doctor. I'm not worried, though my hand has gone numb."

"Are you sure you'll be alright? I mean I can call the doctor. I just want you to be ok."

"There's no need. I'll be fine. I think though I'm going to lay down for a little bit. I think it's the coffee. There's too much caffeine in it."

Harrison goes into the bedroom to lie down. I'm a little concerned for him. I really think that it's not the caffeine. I think Harrison is going to have a stroke or something, but he said he was fine, so I just check on him every hour. I've been writing and getting some work done. I think my book is almost finished. I just have some more to do. It's turned out nicely. I think our trip to South Africa is the best part, and I think it will sell well. Before I know it, it's late afternoon.

The telephone rang. I answered it, and it was Jake.

"Mason, how are you?"

"I am doing great Jake, and you?"

"Fine, thank you. Is Pa there?"

"He is, but he is napping."

"Hmm... Well, I am going to have you wake him up, Mason. I got this sick feeling on my way home from the office and I want to make sure he is okay."

"Sure, Jake, give me a minute."

I place the telephone on hold and walk across the hall and gently open the door. To my surprise Harrison was awake, lying there petting the boys.

"Harrison, Jake is on the phone."

"Ah, I was just thinking about him." Harrison said and I got a chill as I turned to walk out. Then Harrison asked me to have a seat.

Harrison pressed the speaker phone button.

"Jake?"

"Wake up you old fart!" Jake said laughing

"I love you my boy." Harrison said with a deep, sincere and almost strange voice. Jake instantly gasped and I couldn't figure out what was going on.

"NO Pa, NOT NOW, NO!" Jake screamed as his voice cracked into what were definitely tears.

I fixed my eyes on Harrison he motioned for me to approach the bed and reached his hand to my hand.

"I did the best I knew how. I loved deeper than I thought I could. I met me and my soul and I liked what I found. The answers are all found in profound, deep, honest love. If you live from love, you will be alive. Anything else is nothing more than living dead."

My eyes overflowed with tears. Jake said calmly but obviously distraught, "Mason, hug him for me. Hold him with everything you've got!" and I did.

Harrison looked at me and smiled the most beautiful, peaceful and excited smile I have ever seen in my life. It simply lit up the room. He raised his arms out to me and I just collapsed. Jakes voice was cracking but strong.

"They never have to feel that way, because of you and all you gave of yourself Pa."

"Never let them feel that way Jake!" Harrison said in complete confidence and peace.

I leaned up to look at the clock and the time was 5:13, the date of Harrison's birthday. He was gone.

"I scream, "JAKE my GOD, JAKE!"

"It is okay Mason, we are blessed, I will be there shortly." And Jake hung up.

Everything was simply flashing through my mind. The love that Harrison had, the hate that he had experienced and the hope he gave is all I could think about as I looked at his lifeless body.

It was only a couple of minutes before Jake was standing there with me. He had already made the necessary telephone calls. Harrison had this day completely organized in the event it would happen sooner than later.

Jake was beside himself.

"I called Lydia and Olivia; they are on their way from Ohio." Jake said with such emptiness in his voice and simply walked out of the room.

It took no less than a couple of hours before Harrison's body was gone and not much longer after that before the apartment was filled with family and friends. Even Ruthie flew directly from Michigan.

As I walked around the corner to the kitchen and saw them all sitting there, I recalled Harrison saying, "Family belongs in the kitchen." And he just smiled, as he said it. The music was playing. Even though you would catch a glimpse of a tear or a faraway look in their eyes, they were doing exactly what Harrison wanted – they were celebrating life.

Jake hands me a beer and lifting his in the air, looked at me and said, "To love" and everyone lifted their glasses, "To love". You could feel Harrison in the room, there was no doubt about that. So much of Harrison had cracked the doors wide open on life for many of us. He never believed life was meant to be lived within the five senses, but far beyond.

The funeral would not be held for several days. There were too many people traveling into the city. The Odos were coming from South Africa as well. All of us simply did our best to comfort one another. I tried to keep my eyes on Jake, I was concerned for him.

Chapter 39

Deliver Me

The morning of the funeral, I woke up early and had some coffee. The mood in the apartment was quiet and mindfully respectable. At noon, limousines began pulling up in front of the building. Like a freight train moving across a bridge, a never-ending procession of limos stretched for miles down the road. Each family had their own limousine. I even had my own.

As we stepped outside you could feel the weight of the pending ceremony fill the air. My name was called be a coordinator.

When I stepped into the car I saw a black leather box underneath a large bouquet of roses. My name had been etched into the leather case. I opened it to find a solid platinum ring – heavy, solid, and simply, but beautiful. A card was enclosed.

"To Mason, you came into my life to tell my story and within the hour of meeting you, I knew you would become a part of the story itself. ~Thank you Mason. The ring is for family – unbreakable, solid and strong – only you can lose it!"

I slipped the ring onto my finger. I was a complete emotional mess. I desperately tried to fix myself to be presentable before I had to get out of the car at the Cathedral.

There were a lot of people entering the Cathedral. The family was herded together. We were taken in a side door. Every single one of us was wearing a platinum ring and had gotten a personal message and every one of the rings engraves with Harrison's signature. It was a somber moment, but all of us loved the farewell gesture Harrison planned.

We were suddenly asked to stop walking. Lydia turned and then we all turned. Jake had not gotten out of his car, he was alone. Lydia and Olivia walked towards the car and Olivia motioned for me. We all stepped into the car.

Jake was buckled over in overwhelming grief. Harrison was nothing less than his father. He was the only person Jake ever trusted. This sixty something year old man felt as though he had been orphaned again. Olivia reached out for Jakes hand. Jakes ring was not like everyone else's. While platinum, solid and beautiful, it was also containing very masculine and diamonds. Even Olivia was taken back a bit by the size of the diamonds. Lydia then reached out to read the card Harrison had left Jake.

"My son – no father on this earth could be more honored to call you his son. Your journey continues, I have been called home. Never let them feel that way, Jake – you have felt that way – never let them feel that way!" ~ Pa

All of us who saw the note wept heavily. Jake continued to simply repeat: "It all hurts – it all just hurts." All of us tried our best to comfort him.

Finally, we were able to regain enough composure to get into the church. All the other attendees had already been seated.

As we sat in silence, we heard the doors at the back the church open and the heavy sound of the church bell – bong, bong, bong as the casket was carried into the church. With the final ring, we all rose and the song, sung by Sarah Brightman, "Deliver Me" began as the crowd felt tears streaming down their faces. This song composed by Helena Marsh and Jon Marsh in 1998 was a song that Harrison adapted to his life as a prayer.

Deliver me

Out of my sadness

Deliver me

From all of the madness

Deliver me

Courage to guide me

Deliver me

Straight from inside me

All of my life, I've been in hiding

Wishing there was someone just like you

Now that you're here, now that I found you

I know that you're the one to pull me through

My mind swirled as if guided by a tornado, reflecting how this song reflected Harrison's life and what it meant to him.

From that point on the ceremony took on an entirely different feel and tone. The music became empowering, the speeches that were given were a testimony to a life that would never actually stop. Harrison didn't have children of his own. Instead what Harrison did was develop an understanding of a void that so many that he termed his, "lost" needed and did all he could to fill it.

The eulogy was heartfelt and I will include it here:

Harrison sat in front of a hotel in Cleveland, Ohio staring, with tears in his eyes. He had nothing. No money, no clothes but those on his back, no friends and no family that he communicated with. He had a mental illness and was not medicated.

He slept on a bench overlooking the railroad tracks and Lake Erie the night before. He watched as the 'normal and good' people came and went from the hotel. A year prior he was handing his key to the valet at this same hotel and when he retrieved his car that same night, he had three awards in his hands for his work that year. All of the awards started with "The Best" in their description.

The awards were not what Harrison was crying about on that day, however. Nor was the fact he slept on a bench now. In fact, he felt he deserved it all. He had had nothing to eat in five days.

'I don't think the tears were that of sadness, they were tears of complete confusion. I knew I had gifts and talents. I knew I had a purpose in life. I knew I had love in my heart. What I also knew was that I had lost the battle against the demons and felt death was my only choice so that I no longer would hurt and I could no longer hurt anyone else."

At that time in Harrison's life he had come face to face with complete aloneness. By that time he had been imprisoned, emotionally disowned, untrustworthy, raped and now homeless and hungry. He was sick, mentally. He was very sick.

A year prior he had a valet bring his car to him so that he didn't have to walk. On this day, he couldn't walk because his shoes were worn down and his shin splits were too painful.

Harrison sat there the entire day. He didn't spend his time in self-pity but spent his time studying people and their reactions to him. The indifference, the disgust, but most painful were the words of hate. A part of Harrison indeed did die that day.

This is only one picture that I paint. In fact there are many of these times where Harrison killed a part of himself – but what was amazing was how much he lived with what he had left.

Before us lies a man that never forgot humanity. Who, instead of bitterness and a fight of revenge (which he certainly had in him) – he simply said, 'I don't want anyone to feel this way.'

Harrison spent every day of his life with those words influencing everything he did and never lost sight of how he felt that day.

Harrison's life was a living example of a journey. He once said, at the age of 18, 'I want my life to be interesting enough to base a movie on.' That movie could have gone many different ways, but the direction that Harrison took it was to help others.

Harrison's only fear in life was that he would stand before God and God would say, 'I put all these things in your life, right in front of you. I gave you the strength, the spirit, and the talent to do something with them and you ignored them.'

We can safely say, today, that Harrison didn't miss a beat, an opportunity or ever not accept the gifts he was given, regardless of how they were wrapped.

It was interesting, after the eulogy how the air seemed to lift and a sense of responsibility came over me. If there was one thing I had learned from Harrison it was the fact that life truly is about giving, not getting.

Chapter 40

Making Sense of it All

With the funeral events behind us, and the folks in attendance had made their way back to their own families, it was somewhat a relief to simply be in Harrison's apartment in New York, alone. I was making my plans to fly back to Chicago and would finish up the book there.

I stepped out onto the balcony and was brought into the reality that Harrison really was no longer here. Harrison's last words and philosophy continued to pound, like pulse in my mind. 'I never want anyone to feel this way'.

Harrison had once told me, "Another person can never live your experiences and therefore they will never truly know what you have been through or who you are." I felt this overwhelming task of conveying Harrison's experiences in a book. The depth that I experienced during my time spent with him. In reality, I have never come close to the tip of the iceberg; the rest hidden by the ocean.

Harrison once told me that one of the worst things you can do in life is to lie to yourself and be ashamed of the gift that is you. It is so important to laugh at your faults. Very few people out of the 6.5 billion on earth ever intentionally set out to hurt another person. It really isn't natural. Living in shame gets you nowhere – you know who you are and where your heart is – so celebrate it!

Gandhi once said, "To every man, there comes in his lifetime that special moment when he is figuratively tapped on the shoulder and offered the chance to do a very special thing – unique to him and fitted to his talents: What a tragedy if that moment finds him unprepared or unqualified for the work which would be his finest hour."

Even though I never asked, I now know what the secret was that Harrison was hiding. He was hiding from the sadness that filled the early years of his life. He wasn't hiding, in the sense that he was running away or covering up his experiences; rather, he was hiding how they shaped his life. He once made reference to how he took negative feelings and did the opposite of what those feelings were. It wasn't until I received the ring and the note that he left, that I truly understood. His secret was his gift; he could turn the ugly beautiful. It was a power that he had, that others could learn from. It certainly changed me. For years I gave gifts with the expectation of getting; but what I learned is that giving for nothing in return is what the heart of man is made of. It took my journey with Harrison to uncover that key, the secret to life. I felt now that I could leave New York, and carry with me the memory of Harrison.

It will be my goal, through the lessons learned to always make sure that I am indeed prepared and qualified for the day that that tap comes to my shoulder, or has it?

Epilogue

After reviewing my notes, my memories and my experiences with Harrison Remy, I realized that even after nearly 400 pages, I could not possibly capture all the details of Harrison that made him who he was.

The journey of life is certainly the portion of life that stands out as most important – rather than the destination. It is within our journey that we make the choice to learn from the situations. Harrison always said there is one sure fire choice in life and that is: "Do you absorb the 'now' or do you dwell in the past and look to the future thereby ignoring the lesson before you?" Far too many miss this very important instrument of life.

To his last day on this earth, Harrison considered himself a true work in progress. He even interjected a great deal of humor in his process. One quote comes to mind by Robert Frost:

"Forgive me my nonsense. As I forgive the nonsense of those who think they talk sense."

It was this ability to realize his own faults that allowed him to open his heart to those who were struggling with issues that society deemed unacceptable or unworthy of attention. Harrison never concentrated on the system as it was, no matter what great strides they had made in mental health courts or crisis intervention training or even mental health awareness. He concentrated on the voids and the cracks that people were falling through. The only way he could find the true statistics and results of any system was to be with the people that the system affected and that was the information he trusted.

Harrison would read a report and then go into the field to find out if there was a difference. Unfortunately, often times he still found people that were not even touched by the overall machine that was indeed trying to help. Rather than spending time and energy butting against the system – Harrison did all he could to work with it while never letting go of the people that desperately needed the changes. These people were the people that would suffer the consequences of a system that failed them.

There was never any doubt that Harrison was a realist. He understood fully that those that break the law or cross any line society had drawn as unacceptable, needed to have a consequence. However, what Harrison constantly fought for was what that consequence should be.

It never made sense that a mentally ill person that was convicted of a non-violent offense would be sent into a system with those that purposely and violently broke the law. Harrison understood the system quite well. He knew the opportunities and choices that could be made rather than prison. Harrison also understood what recovery was and what effective rehabilitation was.

The argument of cost was simply something Harrison laughed at – because there are not any numbers that reflect that prison is less expensive than rehabilitation. What concerned Harrison more was the human cost that prison took on a person with mental illness and the product that the prison system would eventually release was bound to be worsened than when it was received.

It was during the time that I spent with Harrison Remy that helped Harrison get what he called the 'Aerial View' of his life. It was a cathartic experience to review his life. After his passing, it was Jake that called me and let me know that Harrison led many different lives all wrapped up into one: A series of experiences, some from personality and some from mental illness. There are parts of Harrison's life that were out of his control and parts that he had to find the strength and determination to grow through them. Jake let me know that all the people in Harrison's life as well as Harrison himself are more than willing to open up about those times in his life in an effort to education and bring awareness to mental illness.

What started as one assignment to write about a man has now turned into what will most likely be a long series of assignments and books that delve into the realities of living with mental illness and the challenges that one is faced with. These challenges are both internal and external. The journey is deep and sometimes disturbing, however – it was Harrison's mission and purpose in life to empower those suffering to rise above the shame and self-pity and find empowerment within themselves and all the gifts that they had been given.

The story of Harrison Remy is far from over as we begin to look back through the life a person that has fought and won, fought and lost, and fought and won again – against the silent and invisible demon called mental illness.

You can follow some of Harrison's insights on www.harrisonstory.com. If there are issues that you would like to see discussed, either on the website or in future books please email: askharrison@harrisonstory.com.

Namaste –

Acknowledgments

There are far too many people in this world that I must thank. They need not be thanked for this book, but for the fact that my life is what it is now.

Throughout my life, both good and bad, I have always been blessed with people that delivered the lessons and messages that I needed in my life. I believe this is the case for all of us.

There are some that need special mentioning:

To Deedi, life would not be if it were not for your stable and consistent grounding.

To Terry and Marlene, I started to cry the minute I typed this acknowledgment. You are my earthly example of God. Two people that I can compare my thoughts and reality to and ask myself if this indeed is what God wants.

To Penny, I was before you at one of the worst times in my life. At 120 lbs, disheveled and psychotically depressed. You and I have never stopped learning from one another since.

To Steve, at first you renewed my faith in a system that I condemned and then you renewed my faith in God and friendship.

To my friends Gini and Cyndi, you have allowed me to see myself in a new light that is not attached to the past.

To my lost, the lessons that you taught me are lessons that I will treasure for the rest of my life. Your pain is real and I hear your voice.

To family and friends that managed to see me through behavior and illness without judgment.

And to all of those who have doubted and doubt me, I thank you. If life would have been simple for me – I would have never learned so much from so many.

About the Author

Cory Dobbelaere resides in Northwest Ohio as well as Northern Michigan. This is Cory's first published book and certain to not be the last.

Since leaving prison, Cory has been successful at managing his recovery with Bipolar Disorder. As he had promised himself while living on the streets, he has used the voice he has been given to advocate for the mentally ill and empower those with mental illness to fulfill their dreams.

Cory sits on the Advisory Committee for Mental Illness and the Courts [ACMIC] for the Ohio Supreme Court. He is President of his local Affiliate for the National Alliance on Mental Illness. In 2010, along side a judge and community mental health professionals, he started work on a county mental health mentoring program for the juvenile court.

"When the paradigm in my life shifted from not wanting 'me' to feel that way to not wanting 'anyone' to feel that way – my life began anew."

~ Cory Dobbelaere

cory@harrisonstory.com

www.Harrisonstory.com

CPSIA information can be obtained at www.ICGtesting.com
Printed in the USA
268106BV00001B/19/P